DANGEROUS
DECEPTION

Savannah Stuart

Cover art: Jaycee of Sweet 'N Spicy Designs
Author website: www.savannahstuartauthor.com

Dangerous Deception/KR Press, LLC – 1st ed.
ISBN-10: 1942447175
ISBN-13: 9781942447177

eISBN: 9781942447184

Praise for the books of Savannah Stuart

"Fans of sexy paranormal romance should definitely treat themselves to this sexy & fun story." —Nina's Literary Escape

"I enjoyed this installment so much I'll be picking up book one...worth the price for the punch of plot and heat." —Jessie, HEA USA Today blog

"...a scorching hot read." —The Jeep Diva

"This story was a fantastic summer read!" —Book Lovin' Mamas

"If you're looking for a hot, sweet read, be sure not to miss Tempting Alibi. It's one I know I'll revisit again and again." —Happily Ever After Reviews

"You will not regret reading the previous story or this one. I would recommend it to anyone who loves a great shifter story." —The Long & Short of It

"...a fun and sexy shapeshifter book and definitely worth the read." —The Book Binge

Sage Miller opened the bathroom door and stepped out into the dimly lit bedroom wearing heels and nothing else. If Trent's smile was any indication, she'd chosen the right "outfit".

"I thought you were going to change into something more *comfortable*." He sat up in bed, shoving the sheet off his body, exposing his perfect naked form. He was truly beautiful, though she guessed he'd probably hate that she used that word to describe him. He was all sharp lines and lean muscles.

Her eyes fell to his thick cock. The shiny condom was visible from where she stood. Grinning, she half turned back toward the other room. "I can go put something on if you'd prefer."

"You better get your ass over here," he practically growled.

She placed a hand on her bare hip and walked toward him, devouring the sight of his body, knowing she'd be missing him for a long time to come.

Her nipples immediately tightened and pebbled as his dark gaze swept over her. That was how he'd hooked her into staying with him nearly a week ago. Those damn eyes. Drawing her in like a siren's song.

What was supposed to have been a single night of fun, a way to exorcise her demons and simply *feel* something again, had turned into a week of non-stop sex. The best sex of her life if she was honest. Unfortunately it was about to end.

But not before one more night with him. Because she simply couldn't help herself. She was greedy for more of him.

Slowly, seductively, she moved toward the bed, loving the way he devoured her with his eyes. Until him, no one had never made her feel so treasured, so desired. He looked at her as if he could eat her whole.

As soon as she neared the bed, he grabbed her hips and flipped her on her back before settling between her legs. Looked like he wasn't going to let her tease him.

"Heels on or off?" she asked as she locked her legs behind his back.

"Don't care." He cupped her mound, his gaze pinned to hers as he tested her slickness with his fingers. Groaning, he thrust into her like a man who'd been in prison for the past couple of decades.

The man was insatiable. They'd just finished making love barely an hour ago so her body was primed and ready to go. Her hips rose up to meet his. Wrapping her arms around his back, she met his mouth with a hungry need. She was greedy to get her fill of him.

"Mine," he murmured as he kissed a trail from her jaw to her neck. His dark hair tickled her face as he nipped. "All mine."

For now. She wished it could be for longer, maybe turn into something real. But she was a realist.

When he bent his head to her breast, all coherent thoughts fled. This was the here and now. She'd enjoy their last few moments together.

He circled her hardened nipple with his tongue while he rolled his palm over the other. Gripping his backside with her nails, she drew in ragged breaths at the blissful torture he was inflicting. He'd learned what she liked so quickly.

She was so close to climax, it bordered on pain. Her body was already sensitized from their last bout of sex so it wouldn't take her more than a few minutes. Somehow this man, this virtual stranger, had learned what her body needed to find release in record time. She'd had complaints from former lovers on the amount of time it took her to climax.

Not with Trent. And oddly enough, he didn't feel like a stranger. He was like a long-lost friend.

"Come home with me, Sage," Trent's deep voice reverberated through her as he slowed his strokes.

He pushed up on the bed, his hands caging her in as he moved in and out, bringing her to the brink of orgasm but not giving her what she needed.

"Talk later." She was so close, just a little more and she'd push over the edge. She reached between her legs and started stroking her clit.

"Did I say you could touch what was mine?" he growled. Grabbing her hand, he hooked it with her other wrist above her head and increased his movements. His strokes were hard and steady.

"Then quit teasing and fuck me," she whispered into his ear.

It was like her words set off an atomic bomb. When he resumed his thrusts full force, liquid fire spread through her entire body.

Her nipples brushing against his bare chest was the only other stimulation she needed. In seconds, her inner walls were fiercely clenching around him, pulling him over the edge with her.

They'd never come together before but in that moment, he emitted a loud moan as shudders racked through her body. After a couple more thrusts, he finally collapsed on top of her. Though she didn't want him to move, she eventually pushed against his chest. "You're killing me."

Lightly laughing, he withdrew from her body and rolled over. "Damn," he muttered.

Despite the conflicting thoughts racing through her head, she chuckled. "Damn is right," she murmured in agreement.

He propped up on one elbow to face her. In the dark, his features were fierce, feral and possessive. Internally she squirmed under his intense gaze.

"I meant what I said. Come home with me Sage. You said yourself you're taking a lot of time off work."

She knew that after twelve years of being in the service Trent had just gotten out of the Navy six months ago and was going to visit a friend in New York. She also knew his father was Native American and that he was a machine between the sheets.

What she didn't know, however, was where he lived. And she planned to keep it that way. If he told her, she was likely to look him up later when she was feeling weak and needy.

"Can we talk in the morning?" She traced a finger over his chest, drawing small circles, hoping he'd drop it. She hadn't been entirely honest with him. She wasn't just taking time off, she'd quit her job.

His dark eyes flashed with something she couldn't quite define but he nodded and fell back against the sheets. She curled up next to him but was careful not to entangle too many body parts.

After a decent amount of time had passed, his breathing was steady. Normally he woke up at the slightest sound but they'd had sex three times in the past few hours. The man should be exhausted.

Relief flooded her when the bed didn't creak as she eased off it. She picked up a towel she'd discarded earlier and wrapped it around her body. Her room was directly next to his and she'd already packed her bags.

She risked one last glance at his still figure before quietly slipping out of the room. Thankfully the hallway was empty. She hated leaving like this, like some kind of coward but it was the only way. The man was an addiction she could get used to. And she couldn't afford to let anything or anyone get in the way of her life.

Now that her sister was dead, she was all alone in the world. She owed it to herself to grieve and do all the things they'd always talked about. Having a brief—albeit hot—affair with a man was not in her plans.

And that was all it would be. He wasn't the type of man who did long-term. Even she knew that. What they had was hot but it was only temporary. And she wasn't looking to get her heart broken. Her heart was already in shambles after Marie's death. She couldn't handle having those pieces shattered irrevocably. Trent was the sort of man a woman could fall hard for.

Really hard.

Hell, she wasn't a masochist. As she rolled her suitcase out into the hall, a brief twinge of guilt pinched at her heart but she brushed it away.

He'd be over her in a week. She had no doubt that a man like him would find someone to warm his bed quickly. Her stomach roiled at the thought but this was the choice she had to make. And it was no time for second guessing herself.

CHAPTER ONE

Eighteen months later

Sage glanced up as the bell to the main door sounded. Margo, the secretary, wasn't in yet so she started to rise. Before she'd taken two steps, the door to her private office opened. Immediately she smiled. "Hey, boss. Good to see you here bright and early."

It was barely past seven and her boss rarely made it into the office until nine. Jason Beckman, her boss of six months, gave her a weary smile and dropped a stack of papers onto her desk. "You might not say that once you see what I have in store for you."

She picked up the first batch. Scanning the first few pages, she groaned. "Is that inspector giving you grief again?"

"You got it. Won't sign off on the walk-through unless I get him reservations at Le Coq Au Vin." He rubbed a hand over his face and sighed.

"Is that it?"

"Yeah."

"Then why not just do it for him?" The inspector was a dick but it was easier to just cave to his demands.

"Because I don't want to give in to that corrupt bastard...and because I've tried."

She waved a hand in the air. "My paperwork is piling up thanks to you, so I'll take care of the reservations. When did he want them?"

"Friday." His eyebrows lifted as if he doubted the possibility.

Please.

"Done. Are we still on for the walk-through today?" They were supposed to do the final inspection of one of their biggest warehouses. They'd managed to build a packaging and manufacturing warehouse for one of the top producers of soda in record time. *If* the inspector would sign off on everything.

"Yes but only if—"

"Don't worry about it." She picked up the phone and shooed him away. As he shut the door behind him, she dialed a number she knew by heart. Her friend Chelsea picked up on the third ring.

"There better be a good reason you're calling me so early," she grumbled.

"I have a huge favor to ask... I need a reservation for two this Friday at eight."

"Are you seeing someone and holding out on me?" Chelsea yawned, starting to wake up more. "You better dish now."

"It's not for me. It's for a client." Technically the man wasn't a client but she didn't feel like getting into the dirty details.

"Fine, whose name do you want it to be under?"

"Put it under Jason's name."

"Yum. And how is your sexy boss?" Chelsea practically purred.

Sage inwardly smiled. Jason definitely had that tall, dark and handsome thing going on but she didn't understand why women fawned all over him. The man was totally scatterbrained. He'd forget his head if it wasn't screwed on. "He's good. He asked about you." She added the last part mainly to torture her friend.

"Really?" A loud thump sounded in the background.

"Yes... What was that?"

Chelsea cleared her throat. "Ah, I fell out of bed. Did he really ask about me?" Now she sounded breathless.

"I'll talk to you later." Laughing to herself, she clicked off before her friend could respond. Chelsea was five foot two, had huge breasts, was as adorable as hell and men were always asking about her. It never ceased to amaze Sage that her friend didn't realize what a great catch she was. In the short time she'd known her, it was like Chelsea had a jerk magnet. Maybe she *should* set her up with Jason.

Pulling up her online calendar, she scanned her boss's meetings, making mental notes to remind him. She'd set up a calendar for him and everything was synced to his cell phone but he ignored all of the reminders. Not that she was complaining. The man had given her three raises and she'd only been there half a year. He was brilliant when it came to designing and building but everything else seemed to take a backseat in his brain. Working for him was so different than when she'd been with a multimillion dollar magazine, but she found she liked this better. She liked small town life better too, another surprise.

Just as she pulled out another post-it to stick on his computer—for some reason those reminders tended to work more than his cell phone ones—her door flew open. "Grab your coat. We're heading to the site now."

"Wait...what? I thought we were going this afternoon. I brought clothes to change into." It was a requirement to wear pants, close-toed shoes and hardhats on site at all times.

He gave her a once over. "You're fine. Besides, Sharpe will probably be a lot easier to deal with if you're dressed like that."

She glanced down at herself. Maybe she should be offended by his comment but there was nothing offensive or sexual in the way he said it. Hell, he was probably right. Her pencil skirt was totally appropriate for work and came to her knees but Sharpe was always staring at her legs.

Tom Sharpe was the inspector for most of their jobs within the city limits. Compared to a lot of the people they worked with down at the city, he wasn't bad to deal with. If their work was subpar, there was no way in hell he'd sign off on it, no matter what kind of reservations or gifts they got for him. Deep down, Sage thought Sharpe just liked to give her boss a hard time.

She grabbed her purse and sweater from the hook on the back of her door and followed him. Her peep-toe slingbacks were definitely inappropriate for the job site but somehow she doubted the inspector would care. "Fine, but you're taking me to lunch if that moron hits on me again."

"Then I think it's safe to say I will be. Wait a minute..." He patted his pants pocket and turned back toward his office.

"I've got the punch list in my purse," she said, walking toward the front door.

A blast of fresh fall air hit them as they stepped outside, making her thankful she'd grabbed her sweater. Beckman's Construction Company was located directly in the middle of the growing coastal town. Most of their work was on the outskirts, or neighboring cities but she loved that their corporate office was downtown.

"Heads or tails?" Jason asked as he pulled a quarter out of his pocket.

"Neither. You're driving." Normally they flipped for it but she'd had a sleepless night and didn't feel up to making the trek to the edge of town.

"All right." He pulled out his keys and unlocked his black SUV.

Of course he'd managed to find a spot right in front of the building. She'd shown up half an hour earlier than him and had to park two blocks away. Once she slid into the front seat, he started the ignition but didn't pull away from the curb.

"You forget something else?" She pulled out her keys, ready to head back in.

"No, I just... Is everything all right? I know I'm not supposed to say this to a woman but you look tired. Did you get another phone call or something?"

Sighing, she tossed her keys back in her purse. "Yeah. This time he called my cell phone. It was that same stupid mechanical voice too."

"What did he say?"

"Same as always. 'Your time is coming bitch'. I think it might be a recording or something." She forced her voice to remain neutral, even as a shiver snaked down her spine. At first she'd blown the calls off but now they were coming in with more and more frequency. She'd already called the District Attorney back in New York to make sure the monster they both despised was still in jail. He was but she couldn't shake the unease that maybe these calls weren't pranks.

Jason slapped the steering wheel once, his frustration clear. "I think we need to involve the police. It's been a couple of weeks since all this started and—"

"Can we please talk about this later?" Massaging her temple, she leaned back in the seat. She already had experience dealing with law enforcement and knew there wasn't a damn thing they could do about prank phone calls.

"Fine but this isn't over. Not by a long shot. I can't sit by and do nothing when some maniac could be—"

"I got the builder's risk insurance started for the new plant job. We'll have everything ready in a week or two." Maybe interrupting him and changing the subject would force him to drop it.

He let out a labored sigh but at least he didn't give her any more grief. "This isn't over, but thank you. Oh, you'll get to meet my brother today. He's going to be the foreman on this next one. I told him to stop by the site today so he could meet his new team."

She grinned. "New team as in me?"

"That's right." He chuckled and took a sharp right turn, completely ignoring the stop sign. The man drove like a complete maniac.

"You know, you're going to need to hire someone soon because I can't keep covering the phones in the mornings and afternoons when Margo isn't there."

"I know, I just can't let her go. You know that." Margo worked part-time because she was a single mother, another reason Sage loved working for Jason. He was always trying to help people out.

"I do know that and I agree with you. I'd hate to lose Margo. I think we should hire a high school student to come in during the afternoons. Answering the phones isn't brain surgery and it'll give me a break. The mornings are normally quiet so I can still handle that."

"Hmm. That's not a bad idea. My brother, Trent, might know someone. We can ask him when we get to the site." Jason took another quick turn and Sage nearly lost her breakfast.

Not because of his maniacal driving though. No, she was used to that. "Your brother's name is Trent? I thought his name was Jarod." Her voice shook when she asked but Jason didn't seem to notice.

He shrugged and steered onto the highway. "Trent is the youngest brother. Thought I told you. He's been up in New York for the past year doing some freelance work. I've been trying to get him to move down here and now that I offered him a partnership, he finally took it."

Panic bloomed inside her until reality sank in. Jason's last name was Beckman so it couldn't be her Trent. Well, not *her* Trent but either way, it couldn't be the man who haunted her dreams. Besides, Jason wasn't Native American so there was no way he was related to the man she was thinking about.

Letting the momentary tension ebb from her system, she stared out the window and watched the passing trees. A kaleidoscope of colors flashed past her. A mixture of yellow, orange and reddish hues lined the highway as they sped to their destination.

Sage risked a peek at Jason and shook her head. The man thought of traffic rules as a guideline. One day they were going to take his license away and she'd be stuck chauffeuring him around.

"What?" He glanced at her.

"Nothing. Just thinking that I'll be lucky if I get out of your vehicle alive."

"You sound like my mother." He shook his head as he pulled off the upcoming exit. "We'll be there in a few minutes so don't get your panties in a wad."

"You know, where I come from, talking about panties or any type of female lingerie could be construed as sexual harassment." She reined in a smile.

He shot her a sideways glance. "Bring it up at the next staff meeting and we'll see what the boss says."

"Ha ha."

Steering into the makeshift clay parking lot, he pulled as close as possible to the front entrance. He knew she hated getting her shoes dirty and she couldn't help but smile. He was a little old school and sometimes a bit chauvinistic but the man was thoughtful.

"Thanks." She didn't explain herself because she knew he'd understand.

He grunted in response and jumped from the vehicle.

As they walked under the metal roll-up door, she couldn't help but wonder if his brother was as laid back. She'd been lucky finding this job and hoped the other man was just as easy to work with. Combined with everything she'd gone through the past couple years and now these stupid phone calls, she didn't think she could handle any more complications.

Jason's phone rang the instant their feet hit the concrete floor of the warehouse. "That's Trent. Can you get the inspector started, then go find the owner?"

She nodded and went in search of Sharpe. His truck was outside, so she knew the man was making a nuisance of himself somewhere in the building.

Her heels made a sharp clicking sound as she hurried across the expansive warehouse. She found the inspector behind a stack of packaged bottles, jotting down notes about only God knew what. He was only there to make sure the fire detectors were up to code and the outside elevations were correct. He had no business being back here and she was surprised he hadn't heard her approach considering the racket her heels made

"Mr. Sharpe, good to see you again."

He swiveled from his crouching position and stood at the sound of her voice. His eyes widened slightly but he quickly recovered. "Sage! So good to see you again. And how is the prettiest girl in Hudson Bay?"

"If I see your wife I'll ask her." She couldn't help herself. The man's attitude pissed her off sometimes and once he found out they'd gotten him those reservations, he'd sign off on the report even if she was a smart-ass.

He cleared his throat and had the good grace to look uncomfortable. "Uh, yes, Jason said we'd start inside so—"

"He's on a call so I'll get you started with the fire detectors." She turned and headed back toward the front, forcing him to follow her. He stood about five feet ten but with her three-inch heels, she was a solid inch taller. For some reason, that extra height made her feel powerful, more in control. Just the way she liked it. "Oh, by the way, I managed to swing a reservation at Le Coq Au Vin. Everything's under Jason's name."

He chuckled and shook his head. "I don't know how Jason survived without you."

Nodding politely, she pointed to the east corner of the building. "Think you can manage without me for a second?"

"No problem." Pulling his notepad back out, he turned away.

She retrieved the punch list from her purse and went in search of her boss. She found him outside still on his phone. When he saw her he held up a finger and kept nodding. "All right buddy, I'll see you in a minute."

"Sorry about that. Trent got lost. How's Sharpe doing?"

She rolled her eyes. "Good I guess. I found him snooping behind some crates but he's actually doing his job now."

"Sneaky bastard," he muttered.

"My sentiments exactly." The inspector was a hopeless snoop, but at least he was harmless.

A loud rumbling compelled both of them to turn toward the chain link entrance. "What the heck is that?"

"That would be my brother. His truck needs a new muffler apparently."

"No kidding." A dusty, beat-up looking vehicle careened through the access gate and pulled up on the other side of Jason's shiny SUV.

"You mind sticking around for a second to meet him before you run off to find the owner?"

"Of course not." The owner wanted to do one final run through now that it looked like the inspector was finally signing off on the legal stuff. Tucking the list under her arm, she glanced down at her feet and grimaced. The clay was murder on her new shoes.

Sage glanced at her watch, wondering what was taking Jason's brother so long to get out of his truck. If he didn't hurry, she was going to have to leave. When the door opened and she got a good look at him, she wished she was already gone.

It was *her* Trent. How that was even possible, she didn't know. "*That's* your brother?" The question sounded hoarse and scratchy to her own ears and she doubted Jason missed it.

"Yeah. You know him?" She felt her boss's gaze on her but she couldn't tear her eyes away from Trent.

Broad-shouldered, midnight black hair, perfect bronze coloring and standing about six foot one. He yanked his sunglasses off and stalked toward them. Yep, he still looked good enough to eat. Staring at him now, she couldn't believe she'd ever willingly walked away from him. The man was walking sex appeal.

Heat involuntarily pooled between her legs as his dark eyes roved over her body in a blatantly appreciative manner. She might be fully clothed but the way he stared at her brought back too many memories.

Naked memories.

Another rush of heat slid down her spine. His heated gaze made her feel like he was remembering the same things she was. Her nipples strained painfully against her bra but she was thankful she had one on. At least he wouldn't see the effect he had on her body.

Every instinct she possessed told her to run and hide but that would have been crazy. The man who visited her dreams on a regular basis was walking right toward them. Well, stalking like an angry bear was more like it.

Despite her resolve to stand her ground, she took a small step back as he joined them.

"Sage?" Trent spoke, the deep timber of his voice just as sexy as she remembered.

Somehow she found her voice. Clearing her throat, she said, "Yes. I'm Sage Miller. Nice to meet you." When she held out her hand, he stared at it for a confused moment before enveloping it with his much bigger one. She didn't know why she'd pretended not to know him. The words had just popped out. The thought of explaining to her boss *exactly* how she knew his brother was beyond embarrassing.

After a few seconds, she tried to pull away but he held firm, tugging her a step closer. As if drawn by a magnet, she stared at their clasped hands. His darker skin against her ivory coloring painted an erotic picture. It shouldn't but when she stared at their hands, all she could think about was what their bodies had looked like intertwined. Despite her resolve to stay strong, she could feel heat creeping up her neck. And with her fair skin tone, it had to be obvious.

"Do you two know each other?" Jason asked.

She jerked her hand away, thankful Trent let go. "No."

"Yes," Trent said at the same time.

Out of the corner of her eye, she saw Jason take a few steps back. "Okay then. I'm going to catch up with Sharpe. When you two figure out whether you know each other or not, find me."

As Jason stalked away, she and Trent stared at each other for what felt like an eternity. Though she was sure it was only a few seconds. She broke away first, unable to hold his intense gaze. Yeah, she was a total chicken.

"What the hell are you doing working for my brother?" His harsh words forced her to look up again.

"I uh...I've been working for him for a few months now. I didn't know you were related, I swear. You said your last name was Takoda." This time she held his gaze but shifted under his scrutiny.

"That is my last name. We have different fathers. I thought you lived in New York," his voice deadpanned.

"I did." *Before my sister was murdered.* But, she didn't voice the last part. No sense in bringing that up.

When he didn't say anything, she continued. "Well, I've got to do a final walk through so I guess I'll talk to you later." Her insides were shaking and if she didn't get away from him soon, she was going to be a puddle of mush at his feet. She turned and took a few steps but he stopped her with two words.

"That's it?"

CHAPTER TWO

Trent Takoda stared at the backside of the sexi-est woman he'd ever met. A woman he'd spent months trying to find. To discover she was working for his brother was almost too much irony. He didn't know if he should laugh, cry, or get a drink. Maybe he'd do all three later.

She paused, mid-stride but didn't turn around. "Is that all you have to say?" After the way she'd walked out on him without a word, he wanted an-swers.

Her long, jet-black hair cascaded down her back in perfect waves, drawing his gaze lower. The slim-fitting skirt accentuated her ass perfectly. She was tall, slender, with just enough curves for a man to hold onto. And her sinfully long legs had a little more muscle than he remembered. And he remem-bered them well. Those legs had wrapped around his waist and shoulders so many times he got a hard-on just thinking about it. He shifted his posi-tion but it didn't matter. His balls were pulled so tight, it hurt to move. He couldn't believe he was standing here staring at the woman who played in all his fantasies.

After what felt like an eternity, she half-turned toward him but wouldn't make eye contact. "We'll catch up later."

He gritted his teeth, mainly to keep from saying something stupid. Something he'd only regret seconds later. If she thought she could keep him at arm's length, she was out of her pretty little mind. He'd lost too much sleep over her. Now that he'd found her, he'd be damned if he didn't get some answers.

She hurried away without waiting for him to respond.

"Tell me that's not *her*. Please tell me it's not." His brother spoke as he walked up next to him and slapped him on the back.

"I could but then I'd be lying big brother." Wrenching his gaze away from her ass, he turned to face Jason. "Why didn't you tell me about her?"

"I told you I hired someone new. Didn't realize I needed to send you the backgrounds of everyone in my employ," Jason snorted.

"Have you slept with her?" His brother had never let on that they had that kind of relationship but if they did, Trent might have to kick his ass.

Jason's eyes widened, then his face split into a devious grin. "Hell no. Not saying she's not hot or anything." He held up his hands in defense when Trent took a menacing step toward him. "Look, she's an employee, that's all. The best damn employee I've ever had so don't do anything to run her off."

"Why the hell would you say that?" He ground the words out.

"She ran from you once didn't she?"

Talk about a sucker punch. "You son of a—"

"Listen, all I'm saying is there's obviously a lot you don't know about her so be cautious."

"Do you know something I should?" The thought of his brother being more aware about her life than he was burned a hole in his gut.

He shook his head. "No. I do know that someone hurt her. She alluded to it once but she's a private person. Doesn't date as far as I can tell. Or if she does, she doesn't talk about it."

Trent glanced back across the parking lot but she'd long since disappeared into the two-story building across the way. He understood what his brother was saying about her. When they'd met, he'd sensed a deep sadness in her. Her life force was vibrant though. Anyone in a ten mile radius would have to be blind not to see it but the stark grief he'd seen in her eyes before had been undeniable.

"There's something else." The tone of Jason's voice set off all his warning bells.

He turned back to face his brother. "What?"

"Someone's been bothering her. Harassing calls, that sort of thing. I've been trying to get her to go to the police but she refuses. Says it'll be pointless, that she's dealt with them before with a similar situation. Maybe...hell, maybe she'll listen to you."

Someone was trying to hurt Sage? *His* Sage? Yeah, he'd talk to her and if she didn't listen, he'd put her under lockdown himself.

* * *

Sage packed up her bag and headed for the exit of the school gymnasium. Every Monday she volunteered at Hudson Bay High School to help with their literacy program. She was one of the last tutors to leave for the evening. Normally she enjoyed it but today she couldn't keep her head on straight. And Kyra, the young girl she was helping, had no doubt noticed. Next week she'd make it up to her.

It was dark when she stepped outside and the lights in the parking lot were a joke. Glancing around, she slipped her pepper spray and keys out of her purse and hurried across the lot. When she'd arrived it had been full but now it was dark and virtually empty and of course her little car was isolated near a cluster of trees.

"Just great," she muttered under her breath.

As she neared the vehicle, a shadow stepped out from one of the trees. She tensed, ready to use her pepper spray until she realized who it was.

Heart beating erratically, she marched over to Trent. She poked a finger into his chest, her entire body trembling from the adrenaline rush she'd just experienced. "Are you trying to give me a heart attack? What the hell are you doing lurking around here like some kind of weirdo?" She hated that her voice trembled, but he'd scared her.

He lifted his big shoulders once, obviously not the least bit apologetic. "There was some guy hanging around here earlier and I just wanted to make sure you made it to your car safely."

"Oh… thank you. But you still didn't answer my question. What are you doing here? And how did you even know I'd be here?"

"I think that much is obvious. You left the office today before we could talk. It didn't take much to convince Jason to tell me where you'd be." His deep voice enveloped her like the sweetest caress.

God, she'd missed him. Staring up at him, she realized she'd flattened her palm against his chest and he wasn't making a move to step away.

Common sense said she should walk away now but her body just reacted around him. Against all reason. The man was like a drug. Leaning forward, she inhaled, savoring his masculine, dark scent. She couldn't quite describe it but he had a smell that was all him; earthy and sexy.

Without thinking, she fisted his shirt, feeling his muscular chest against her hand. She'd kissed that chest too many times to count. They'd only spent a week together but it had been the best week of her entire life. It was impossible to believe he was standing in front of her again. She'd never thought she'd see him again.

He advanced, his features positively feral and possessive under the dim lighting. On instinct, she took a few steps back.

"What are you doing?" she breathed out as her back and legs hit the car. She wasn't sure why she asked when she knew exactly what he was doing.

"Catching up," he murmured and tucked a way-ward strand of hair behind her ear.

Her nipples strained painfully against the sheer bra, reminding her of everything he could do to her body. She stared at his lips, wondering how she'd ever walked away from him. Momentary insanity. That was her only defense.

"Why'd you leave, Sage?" He leaned down and nipped her earlobe, his deep voice an aphrodisiac, caressing her skin.

"Hmm?" She arched her back, needing to feel his body against hers. Automatically, she spread her legs as far as the restrictive skirt would allow. More than anything, she wanted to wrap her legs around him. Feel him against her body again.

Feathering kisses along her jaw, he didn't stop until he found the sensitive spot on her neck, just above her collarbone.

They were right out in the open, for anyone to stumble upon. The thought registered in her brain but she quickly dismissed it when his finger delved under her blouse. Unable to look away, she watched as he popped open two buttons with one hand. Tracing along the edge of her lace bra, he probed under the cup. He raked a finger along the sensitive skin until he finally shifted the covering away.

Cupping her breast, he rubbed her nipple in small, erotic circles. "Sage?" He spoke near her ear again as he popped the rest of the buttons free, completely opening her blouse with his other hand.

Then, he unclasped the front hook, freeing her breasts. Exposing her.

She shivered as the cool air washed over her. Her nipples tightened into hard buds, but it had nothing to do with the weather. "What?" she murmured. How he could think or talk now, she couldn't understand. His cock strained against his jeans, pushing up against her lower abdomen. She'd missed the feel of him thrusting inside her.

His hands might be calm but she knew he was just as turned on as she was. And they really needed to find somewhere private. "We need privacy," she said. Because what she wanted to do with him, they couldn't do in a semi-public parking lot.

"Come on sweetheart, tell me why you left."

"No talking." Shifting against him, she wiggled her skirt up a few inches.

He didn't need another incentive. He bunched her skirt up around her waist. She was already soaked and when he traced a finger along the edge of her panties, she thought she'd come right there. Right in the parking lot of the local high school. She should probably be more embarrassed by that, but couldn't muster any shame. Not when Trent had her pressed up against the car like this.

He cupped her mound, then moved the thin shred of material away. One finger probed gently while his thumb massaged her clit. It was too much and too little at the same time. Her body screamed for release but he was taking his time. Grinding against his hand, she tried to force him to increase his tempo. He knew what she liked, had played with her body enough times to know how to make her climax in minutes.

"Tell me why you left." This time his words were more demanding. And his caresses less gentle. He withdrew his hand from her slick body and moved to her breasts. A little roughly, he pinched and palmed her nipples as he crushed his mouth over hers. She'd missed his kisses. More than she should have. As he tugged on her bottom lip with his teeth, she moaned aloud and arched into him again. They needed to find a more private place or she was going to let him take her up against the car.

"Talk later. We need to go somewhere private," she muttered, her eyes half closed as she pressed up against him. She wanted him inside her. When she linked her fingers together behind his neck, he grabbed her ass, tugging her even tighter against him. Instinctively, she wrapped a leg around him, rubbing her swollen clit over the fabric of his jeans, trying to pull him closer.

Oh yeah, this was what she'd been missing the past year and a half. Way too long to go without sex. Fumbling, she reached for his belt. She couldn't wait any longer. And it wasn't like she worked at the school. At least that's what she told herself as she shelved all embarrassment. Maybe she'd regret this later, but it was hard to feel anything but need and hunger at the moment.

He pulled his head back and immediately she missed the warmth of his mouth. "You feel what you do to me?" he growled.

Mutely she nodded as he took a step back. Her leg fell and immediately she felt exposed and a little vulnerable. He couldn't be stopping now. "What are you doing?"

"Tell me why you left, damn it." Breathing heavily, he crossed his arms over his chest.

"What?"

But he stood there. Immovable with hints of anger etched on his handsome face.

Gritting her teeth, she yanked her skirt down and tugged her shirt together to cover her breasts, then turned her back to him. She didn't bother to button her top. The only thing that mattered was getting out of there.

Embarrassment flooded her veins. How could she have let him get under her skin so quickly? They'd almost had sex up against her car. Hell, she was still turned on and willing. Pathetic.

"Sage, listen—"

She shrugged his hand off her shoulder and jumped in the front seat. Clearly frustrated, he tapped on the window but she slammed the locks into place. She couldn't believe he thought he could use sex to get what he wanted. More than anything, she was angry at herself for letting things go so far. He'd turned her on within seconds and hadn't given her a release and now all she could think about was letting him finish what he'd started. Which made her feel even more pathetic.

"Bastard," she muttered as she started the ignition.

"Damn it Sage, open the fucking door." She could see him in her peripheral vision but wouldn't give him the satisfaction of looking at him.

He knocked on the window again, harder this time, so she kicked the car into drive and steered out of her spot. Through the rearview mirror she saw him jog toward a truck. It wasn't the same vehicle he'd driven earlier that day or she would have recognized it. She didn't think he was crazy enough to follow her home but past experiences had taught her that she was a bad judge of character.

Gunning her engine, she peeled out of the parking lot and took a few random side streets before heading back downtown. She lived in a town house right in the heart of the small town center. Sometimes she missed the noise and bustle of living in New York but her current home reminded her of the town house she'd shared with her sister.

As she drove down her street, her heart jumped when she saw a prime parking spot. Usually she had to walk a few blocks but she found one right in front. Hudson Bay balked at building parking garages in their historic downtown and she really couldn't blame them. After adjusting her clothes, she grabbed her purse and rushed up the few steps to the front door. When she tried to slide the key in the lock, the bright red door swung open.

A shiver of unease ran down her spine. She always locked her doors. Hell, she was obsessive about it. Glancing around the quiet block, she clutched her purse a little closer and bolted down the sidewalk. Running in heels felt ridiculous but if someone had broken in, she wasn't going to stick around. Just around the corner was a coffee shop and they were open for at least another hour. Once inside and around people, she dialed her friend Chelsea.

When it went straight to voicemail, she chewed on her bottom lip. She didn't want to call the police before she knew anything and waste their time. And she couldn't risk going inside by herself. She refused to end up a statistic because of a stupid decision. After dialing Chelsea again with no luck, she bit the bullet and called Jason. She knew he'd freak out and probably call the National Guard but she didn't have a choice unless she wanted to sleep at Java Joe's.

He picked up on the third ring. And he sounded out of breath. "Sage? Is everything okay? Why are you calling so late?"

"Uh... I think someone might have broken into my house and—"

"Don't go inside!"

She rubbed her temple. "I know. I'm around the corner at Java Joe's and—"

He cut her off again. "Stay there. And keep your phone close."

Before she could respond, he hung up. After a few minutes passed and he didn't call back, she ordered a hot green tea. Some of her nerves had eased, but not by much. Just as she was sitting down at one of the high top tables, Trent walked in. Well, marched toward her like a general was more like it. His dark eyes were unreadable but he was homing in on her like a heat-seeking missile.

"What are you doing?" Nervous, she stood as he neared the table.

His expression was annoyingly neutral. "Jason called me."

"Oh." Well crap. She hadn't counted on that.

"Have you called the police?"

She shook her head.

Without giving her a hint of what he intended, he slid his cell phone out of his front pocket and punched in a number. At first she assumed he was calling his brother back but after a few seconds into the conversation she realized he must have a friend on the police force.

"Who was that?" she asked after he hung up. She'd heard most of the conversation but it was one-sided.

"Sergeant Steve Graybar. He's an old friend of mine and he's in the neighborhood. He'll be at your place in sixty seconds. We can meet him there."

She should be grateful he was helping her out. Instead, annoyance bubbled up at his commanding attitude. She knew that was more because she was stressed than anything, but it still rankled. "Why did Jason call you?"

"He was at...a friend's house. He knew I'd gone to see you this evening so he guessed I'd still be close. So, you want to walk back to your place?"

"How do you know where I live...never mind." Of course Jason must have told him. She'd have a few choice words for her boss later.

As if he read her mind, he said, "Jason told me you were here. I didn't see your vehicle in the parking lot so I figured you live close."

She picked up the to-go cup and slung her purse over her shoulder. Without waiting for him, she strode from the small establishment. It was a little rude but she couldn't help it. Being near him put her on edge and she'd about reached her limit for the day.

Trent fell in step next to her as they headed down the sidewalk toward her place. At least he didn't try to make small talk. She didn't think she could handle social niceties right now. As they reached her place, a police car was parking. Thankfully, the lights weren't flashing. She didn't want to draw attention to herself from her neighbors.

One of the two police officers immediately got out of the car and strode toward them. Despite the circumstances, he grinned when he looked at Trent.

His nametag read Sergeant Graybar. "Good to see you man. Didn't know you were back in town."

Trent's mouth curved up in what she knew to be his version of a smile as he held out a hand to him. "Good to see you too. We'll have to grab a beer later this week."

The man nodded, then turned his attention to her. "I'm Sergeant Graybar but you can call me Steve. I take it you're Sage?"

She cleared her throat and glanced uncertainly between him and Trent. "Yes. This could all be a mistake but when I got home and the door wasn't locked, I didn't want to go inside."

"You did the right thing. You two stay out here okay," he ordered. Not that she was inclined to argue.

"I won't let her out of my sight," Trent said quietly.

As Graybar and a man she assumed was his partner disappeared inside, she blew out a long breath. "Look, I'm sorry if I was rude earlier. I really do appreciate you coming over." The thought of dealing with cops again by herself brought up too many painful memories.

She didn't consider Trent a permanent part of her life or anything but it was nice to have a strong presence with her. He simply nodded and grunted a response that could have meant anything.

A couple of minutes later, the men exited. By the grim expression on both their faces, she didn't want to guess what was inside.

"Uh, Trent..." Steve motioned to him, silently asking him to come inside while completely ignoring her.

Uh, hello? This was her house. Annoyed, she followed Trent up the steps. He frowned when he realized she was right behind him but didn't say anything. When they got to the front door, he moved back so she could pass and placed his hand at the small of her back as they walked in.

The front door opened into a foyer but immediately to the left was a sitting room. Steve spared her a concerned look before gesturing to the room. When she walked in, she wondered what he was so worried about until she turned to the right.

Across the periwinkle blue accent wall she'd painstakingly painted herself, written in a garish crimson color was the word "whore". The paint dripped down across her pictures and onto the hardwood floor, creating a horrific display. Her stomach rolled once and she automatically took a step back, right into Trent's strong embrace. She welcomed it when he placed steadying hands on her hips.

"Come on." He led her back to the foyer.

"Is there anything else?" she rasped out, a low grade panic humming through her.

"We don't know yet," Steve said.

"How do you not know?" she asked.

"Are you a messy person?"

"Not really, why?"

"Well, your room. It's ah…"

Pushing away from both of them, she raced up the stairs. She could hear them close behind but the rush of blood in her ears thundered louder than anything.

Her bedroom door was open but she halted in the doorway. Clothes were strewn everywhere, her lingerie drawer had been tossed but something else drew all her attention. The picture of her and her younger sister, which normally sat on her nightstand, was face down on the floor.

Aware of the two men behind her, she took a few steps inside.

"Careful, you could disturb evidence." Steve ordered.

She doubted it. The person who had done this was smart. Too smart to leave behind fingerprints or anything else. She pointed to the frame and looked at Steve. "Can I pick this up?"

"I'll do it." He picked up one of her discarded shirts and used it to cover his fingers as he lifted the frame up by the edge.

Ice slid through her veins when he turned it over. Written across the glass in her red lipstick were the words "you're next". All the muscles in her body tightened. It couldn't be the same man. It just couldn't. He was still in jail.

Trent let out a low curse when he saw what it said. Steve's expression was grim as he set the frame on her nightstand.

"Is she related to you?" He stared at the picture, then looked back at her.

The woman in the picture was about half a foot shorter and more delicate in appearance but it was obvious they were related. Her jaw clenched and she forced back tears. Now wasn't the time to completely break down. "Her name's Marie. She was my sister."

"Was?"

She nodded. "She was murdered."

* * *

He'd finally found her. After she'd left New York it was as if the bitch had fallen off the face of the earth. He'd known she was out there though, had been able to feel her through their connection all this time. The connection she wanted to deny. Almost two years later and he was finally going to claim who was his.

Sage.

He balled his hands into fists as he watched the commotion going on at her town house. He wasn't sure why she'd thought she could run from him. Foolish, foolish female. No one said no to him, embarrassed him the way she had. Fucking tease. He'd have hunted her down a month ago when he first learned where she'd been living, but he'd been out of the country for work. The taunting phone calls had been fun though, had revved him up enough that he'd been dying to get to her. So much so that even his work had suffered on the last shoot. His heart simply hadn't been in it.

For so long he'd loved his job, but even that didn't hold the same appeal it used to. Not since everything had gone wrong, since Sage had disappeared. *Left him.*

The anticipation of waiting to see her again in the flesh had been worth it.

No more stroking himself off to pictures of her. He had so many to choose from, but it wasn't the same as the real thing. And it wasn't as if she had any social media accounts he could follow either. She'd deleted all of those when she'd left New York too. Like she wanted to erase her entire past.

He wasn't going to let her though.

Remaining cloaked in the shadows across the street, he watched as a big man stepped out of Sage's town house and strode down the steps. Even from where he was, he could see that the guy was pissed. It was clear in the tense way he moved. Must have seen the present he'd left for Sage.

He got hard just thinking about how he'd stroked her panties, all her things. He'd stolen two pairs, had them both in his pocket. Later he'd rub them over his cock, find release in them. He would have taken more of her belongings, but there hadn't been enough time.

After seeing Sage moaning and rubbing up against that fucking nobody down at the high school he'd lost it. It had been potentially foolish to break into her house since he hadn't had time to do enough recon, but he'd been impatient and angry. He'd needed to hurt her after the way she'd hurt him. She shouldn't have kissed that guy, let that bastard grope her up against her car for anyone to see.

Fucking slut.

That was all she was. Her sister had been one too, but he'd enjoyed her. Had enjoyed making Marie scream and cry. Though she hadn't begged enough for his liking. She'd been defiant and angry right to the end.

He wondered if Sage would be defiant or if she'd beg him to stop. He hoped it was both. He wanted to break her, to take everything from her.

He shifted farther back against the brick wall of the town home across the street, not wanting anyone to inadvertently see him. There weren't any outside lights illuminating him, but across the street he saw curtains being pulled back in a few of Sage's neighbors' windows. Well that was good to know.

At least his break in hadn't been wasted. Her neighbors were nosy enough, but not so curious that they came out to see what was going on when there was a police car in front of her place.

Now he also knew she didn't have a security system. He hadn't been able to tell until he'd broken in.

When she stepped outside with a uniformed police officer, hunger surged through him as he drank in the sight of her. There she was, afraid and beautiful. Just like he remembered.

He would have treated her like a queen, but she'd wanted nothing to do with him. Tall and lean with perfect tits, she had a face he loved to photograph. He'd had to do it when she wasn't aware though. Sometimes he would stare at her pictures for hours. He hated and loved what she did to him, the power she had over him.

Soon enough he would have all the power over her, would make her beg for her life, make her beg for his cock. And he would take so many pictures. Before he'd had to be satisfied with covert shots, but he'd get all of her, every naked inch.

Even thinking about that, his dick started to get hard. He rubbed a gloved hand over the front of his pants once, twice... he had to stop.

Shaking himself, he stepped farther back into the shadows. It was time to go. He might want to stay and watch her, but he'd come this far. It wouldn't do for him to screw up now.

He already knew where she worked so it didn't matter where she went tonight. She might stay at her place, but he doubted it. She wouldn't want to be around his handiwork. He'd follow her from work later, find out where she was staying, *who* she was staying with.

It would probably be that tall bastard who'd raced to her rescue. She could just be teasing him, but it hadn't looked like it at the school. No, she'd given that guy what he'd wanted. He would have to die too for touching Sage, touching what belonged to him and him alone.

Maybe he'd make her watch.

Thinking of that made his smile grow as he crossed the tiny backyard and jumped a fence into another equally small backyard. He'd parked a street over so his getaway wouldn't take him long.

Patience, he reminded himself. He just had to be patient and soon everything he wanted would be his.

CHAPTER THREE

Trent's gut tightened at Sage's words. The thought of losing any of his brothers was unimaginable. As he watched Sage, he could almost see her pulling inside herself. Blocking out the rest of the world. The most primal part of him wanted to reach out and comfort her. Nurture her. Take care of her because she was his.

His brain, however, told him now wasn't the time. Her skin had paled to an almost ashen gray and she looked ready to fall apart at any moment. Her jaw clenched furiously while she tried to hold back tears. Damn it, he wanted to pull her into his arms, but knew she needed to gain control. Something he understood.

Steve cleared his throat. "You're going to need to file a report. And we'll need to go over how long you've been living here, any enemies you think could have done this, any ex-boyfriends who might want to exact revenge for a breakup. *Anyone* you can think of, we'll need to know."

She quickly glanced at Trent and he wasn't sure what was going on inside that pretty head but she looked back at Steve when she answered. "I've been living here for about six months and I've been on a few dates but nothing serious."

A knife twisted inside him at the thought of her dating but he pushed them away. Or he thought he did.

The blade screwed even deeper when Sage spoke again. "If you don't mind Trent, I'd like to talk to Sergeant, uh, Steve alone about this."

Steve nodded once at him, telling him he needed to leave. Swallowing his annoyance, Trent nodded. "I'll be downstairs if you need me. Tell him about the phone calls you've been receiving."

She blinked, clearly surprised he knew about the calls. Just as quickly, her lips pulled into a thin line as it registered that Jason must have told him.

Trent pulled out his cell phone as he left the room and dialed an old friend. Other than his two brothers, Trent had a handful of men he called friends and they were all from his time in the Navy. Most lived scattered across the country but thankfully a few were located in North Carolina. After twelve years in the service, he'd retired two years ago. But he'd stayed in contact with his old teammates and hoped one of them could help him out. Some were still in the service but almost everyone who had retired was in some sort of law enforcement.

Everyone but him. If he never had to take another human life, it would be too soon.

He'd met Sage barely six months after he got out of the Navy but she'd disappeared before they could truly get to know one another. He thought he'd known her. Hell, he thought he'd known everything a man needed to know about a woman when he'd met her but tonight's revelations had been a rude awakening.

Sighing to himself, he walked outside and sat on the front stoop. The phone had rung four times and he was about to hang up, when his friend picked up.

"Tell me you don't need bail money," Eli Romero said by way of greeting.

A smile tugged at his mouth. "If I did I wouldn't be calling your cheap ass."

After a few minutes of bullshitting, his friend finally gave him an opening. "What's up man?"

"I need a security system for a friend of mine. It's residential, so I know it's not normally your thing but I want the best." Eli was owner and founder of

Romero Security. He lived in Wilmington, a few hours south and while he normally set up large, commercial accounts, Trent knew he'd come through for him.

"What's her name?"

No surprise Eli had guessed it was for a woman. "Sage."

"No problem. Email me the details and I'll get a guy on it. Two days max."

"Thanks. I owe you one."

After they disconnected, he moved from his sitting position to lean against Sage's car. The other officer had come back outside and was on the radio, presumably to get backup to catalog and investigate the crime scene.

Feeling useless, Trent scrubbed a hand over his face. He wanted to be doing something. *Anything.*

When Sage and Steve walked out, he shoved up from the car. She was rolling a large suitcase and had a smaller travel kit stacked on top of it. Good, at least she wasn't going to be stubborn and insist on staying at her place. He didn't know that she'd be able to anyway until they cleared her house.

Steve handed her a card, then leaned in closer than was appropriate, at least in Trent's mind. He said something too low for Trent to hear. On pure instinct he took a few steps forward, then tempered his anger. Acting like a jealous asshole wouldn't do anything to help Sage right now. The other man nodded at him, then pulled out his cell phone. Sage walked toward Trent, a little uncertainly, until she stood next to her car.

"They're getting someone down here to look at the crime scene, but said I could make a report in the morning."

He was surprised by that, but glad. She needed to get out of here and get some rest. Pale circles ringed under her eyes and she looked ready to fall over.

"Thank you for coming here with me," she continued. "I'll be finding a hotel so you can rest easier."

"The hell you are." He didn't bother hiding his anger. "You'll stay with me."

She blinked in surprise—and the fact that was actually surprised by his offer, pissed him off. "That's a sweet offer, but I don't think it's a good idea."

"It's a great idea. At least until your security system is installed." He took a step forward and retrieved her suitcase as she stared at him. She didn't even protest. He guessed because she was too stunned.

"Security system? I haven't had a chance to call anyone." She rubbed a hand over the back of her neck, her clear exhaustion making all his protective instincts surge up and take over.

"That's okay, I already took care of it. I called a friend and he'll be sending someone out this week. He's the best, trust me."

She blinked in surprise. "You can't just barge into my life and start making decisions." There wasn't much heat behind her words, just weariness.

He didn't bother responding to that. Right now she needed to get out of here and get some rest. "Do you need anything else or are you ready to go?"

"Damn it Trent, I am ready to leave but I'm not going anywhere with you. I don't want to put you in danger." She moved to grab her suitcase but he sidestepped in front of it. Now if she wanted her things, she'd have to touch him. And he knew she wouldn't. Not after what had happened earlier in that parking lot.

She placed manicured hands on slim hips. "Move."

"I can but if you go to a hotel, I'm just going to follow you and stay in the next room." When she didn't respond, he continued, "What happened in there isn't a typical prank. Especially not considering those phone calls you've been receiving. You know it and I know it. You need me."

She stared at him for a few long seconds. He could see the exact moment when she made the decision to give in. Her green eyes flickered with resignation and a little relief. He guessed she didn't mind the idea of staying with him as much as she wanted him to think. "Fine. I'll stay for *one* night. And I'm sleeping by myself."

Yeah, we'll see about that. He could see in her eyes she didn't quite believe her own statement.

The drive to his place was quiet. He wanted her to open up to him, but he guessed she needed to mentally regroup. He could give her that space for now. Something told him she had an idea who might be behind what had happened. She'd been shocked but she'd also handled things uncommonly well. He'd probe deeper later. Now all he cared about was getting her into the safety of his house.

And his bed.

He lived a few minutes outside the city limits, right on the beach so the drive didn't take long.

As he steered down his street, she broke the silence. "What happened to that other truck you were driving?"

He glanced at her. She was turned away from him, staring out the passenger window, but at least she was talking.

"It's at my house. It's my work truck."

When she didn't continue, he decided to push. "So what did Steve say to you as you were leaving?"

She looked at him now, her cheeks tinged pink. "Nothing." Clearly a lie. But when he shut off the ignition, she unsnapped her seat belt and jumped out.

They weren't done with this conversation though. After retrieving her bags, they walked to the front door in silence. He inserted the key in the lock but didn't open the door.

"What's wrong?" Startled, she looked up at him, her green eyes appearing almost black in the dim light.

"Did he ask you out?" Trent didn't know why he was pushing. Now wasn't the time but the way she'd blushed gnawed at him.

She chewed on her bottom lip for a long moment. "He asked if I was dating you and when I said no, he gave me his phone number."

Steve had a lot of fucking nerve but he'd deal with that later. "You're not dating him." He twisted the lock and stepped inside before clearing the way for her. He dropped her bags right next to the front door.

She followed him into his foyer and swiveled to face him as he shut and locked the door. "I appreciate what you're doing right now but you don't have any say over my life."

"That's where you're wrong." He set his alarm system to stay mode before turning to her.

He had to play this right. If he didn't make a move now, she'd have time to think about whatever it was that had chased her off before. And he wasn't making the same mistake twice. He'd run through their last night together a million times in his head and he realized he must have done something to scare her. When he'd asked her to come home with him, he hadn't given her a reason. Hell, he technically hadn't asked, he'd ordered. Now that she was in the same zip code, he was getting her into his bed and keeping her there. He might hate the circumstances that had brought her under his roof, but he wasn't letting her go.

He slid his fingers through the curtain of her dark hair and cupped her head. In her heels, she was only a few inches shorter than him. She tried to pull back but he refused to budge. Her eyes narrowed and instead of pulling away this time, she leaned forward until their faces were almost touching. "I'm not answering any questions tonight Trent so you can forget it. I just... can't. I don't have the energy."

"Talking is the last thing on my mind," he murmured.

Surprise and something hot flared in her eyes. He knew he'd been an idiot back at the school but she'd been inside his head for the better part of the last year and a half. Now all he cared about was getting inside her and easing that ache. Or at least dulling it so he could think straight.

Her breathing was just as labored as his, her breasts rubbing against his chest and making him crazy. She watched him carefully, a mix of emotions in her eyes. Waiting for him to make a move? He couldn't decide. At least she wasn't telling him to stop.

He flicked his gaze down to her blouse and another wave of lust swept through him. It took all his self-control not to tug her blouse open and take her right then. She needed to let him know she wanted it though. She'd been dealing with a lot and he didn't want to take advantage.

Her hands tentatively moved to his belt but they stilled at the button of his jeans. "You swear you're not going to get me all hot and turned on, then stop?"

He might want answers but he could wait. "We're not stopping unless you say, sweetheart."

Tension eased from her shoulders. "Then let's finish what you started earlier," she whispered.

"Hell yes." She didn't have to tell him twice. Wrapping his arms around her waist, he promptly unzipped her skirt. No way was he pushing it up this time. He wanted to see every single inch of her. Including her sexy-as-sin legs. Tall and lean, he loved everything about her body. The skirt pooled at her feet before she kicked it away.

He slid his hands down her back and over her ass. He squeezed when he reached the part her bikini-cut panties didn't quite cover. Her skin was silky smooth, just like he remembered. When she grabbed onto his shoulders, he hoisted her up so that she wrapped her legs around him. Driven with the need to get inside her as quickly as possible, he headed for the stairs.

"What are you doing?" There was a sudden undertone of panic in her voice.

Even though he wanted nothing more than to fuck her up against that wall, on the floor and the couch, this time was going to be in his bed. He wanted to do too many things to her body that required a comfortable surface—and she deserved a bed after the day she'd had. "Just taking us upstairs." He brushed his lips over hers before nipping her bottom lip between his teeth.

Relaxing against him, she let out a pleasured sigh as he carried her up the stairs.

Seconds later they were in his room. He didn't bother with the lights. His blinds were turned slightly open, giving them enough illumination from the moon and stars. Feeling practically possessed, he set her on the edge of the bed and just looked down at her.

She stretched out for him, looking like a pagan offering as she spread her legs. Long, dark hair pillowed around her, her breathing as erratic as his. The only problem was, she still had clothes on. As if she read his mind, she moved into action. She tugged off her sweater, unbuttoned her shirt and slid it and her bra off. Leaving only her panties and heels on.

Without warning she kicked her shoes off and his cock jumped. He'd wanted to give her plenty of foreplay but that wasn't going to happen. Not the first time.

She leaned back on her elbows and stared at him with a hungry look he remembered well. The bare grip on control he'd had, snapped. He stripped off his own clothes in record time. She hitched in a breath as her gaze landed on his fully erect cock.

Grabbing her ankles, he pinned them to the mattress. Consumed with the need to taste all of her, he raked his teeth and tongue over her inner calves and thighs, moving his way up her delectable body. Hell, he'd been thinking about this all day since seeing her.

Longer than that actually. He deserved a fucking medal for what he did at the school. Or a kick in the ass. If he hadn't restrained himself, he'd have been with her when she got home. No, he mentally shook his head and reached up to grip her hips. He wouldn't think about that right now. Not when she deserved all his attention.

She let out a little yelp when he grabbed her.

"You're so fucking beautiful woman," he murmured against her leg.

Not exactly poetry but coming from Trent, Sage knew he meant every one of those words. And she desperately needed to hear them. An unexpected shudder raked through her body as his mouth moved over her bare skin with skill. She hadn't realized how much she'd needed this kind of release until now. When she was with Trent, the outside world ceased to exist. And she actually felt safe.

It was an illusion but she'd indulge for the night. After that, however, she was walking away from him. For his own sake. She couldn't bring all this baggage and trouble down on his head. He didn't deserve it.

"Trent." She moaned out his name when he pushed her panties to the side and sucked on her clit. The abrupt tug shocked all her senses, sending spirals of pleasure to all her nerve endings as he flicked his tongue over the sensitive bundle of nerves. She nearly vaulted her off the bed when he sucked again. "Oh… just like that."

She dug her fingers into his shoulders, gripping him, begging him to finish what he started this time. If he didn't, she'd kill him.

He lifted his head and she didn't miss the satisfied, male grin tugging at the corners of his mouth. He knew exactly what he was doing to her. Her inner walls tightened when he yanked the last shred of material separating them down her legs. She knew what was coming and couldn't wait to feel him inside her, thrusting and taking.

When he moved on top of her, she shivered in anticipation. His dark hair was longer than she remembered and when he slanted his mouth over hers, it tickled her face, the light brushing only adding to her heightened sensations.

Arching her back, she rubbed her breasts against his chest, savoring the feel of skin on skin. God, she'd missed him. So damn much. His lips teased and caressed hers, while one hand worked its way between their intertwined bodies. "Condom," she murmured against his mouth.

He lifted his head. "I was trying to give you a little foreplay."

"Screw foreplay." She dug her hands into his backside and gripped the firm muscles. Her body had been ready to go hours ago. She was completely soaked just thinking about what it would be like to have him inside her again.

His midnight eyes seemed to darken as he leaned over and retrieved a condom from the dresser drawer. He used to like her to roll it on but he ripped into the foil and sheathed himself before she could blink.

"Are you ready?" For some reason, his words sounded ominous, dangerous and a whole lot sexy. She knew what she was getting herself into though.

This was only the beginning of the night for them. Sex with Trent had always been hot and intense. The first time he'd fuck her fast and furiously, almost like he needed to prepare himself. Then, they'd make love for hours.

He lifted one of her legs and positioned it over his shoulder. She shivered at the sensation of being so open for him. Kissing her ankle and inner calf, he poised himself at her entrance.

Without giving him a chance to tease her, she shifted her hips, partially impaling herself on him. Wet and slick, her body gratefully accepted him. For a split second, his eyes widened but then he took her other leg and looped it over his other shoulder before completely thrusting into her.

The abrupt intrusion bordered on painful but quickly turned to pleasure. In this position, she could handle him as deep as she wanted, something he already knew.

Tracing her hands over her breasts, she rolled and pinched her nipples, caressing herself until they were rock hard and aching with pleasure.

Using muscles she'd forgotten she had, she lifted her hips, meeting him stroke for stroke. Her inner walls clenched around him tighter and tighter with each thrust. Her climax was coming hard and fast.

And so was his. She could feel him about to break. He gripped her hips so tightly she knew he'd leave bruises.

The thought of being marked by him sent another rush of pleasure through her.

She tried to keep her eyes open, wanting to watch him come but when he reached down and teased her clit with his thumb, she pushed right over the edge, surging into climax. It happened so fast she wasn't prepared for it.

Head thrown back against the bed, she grasped the sheet as if it could somehow ground her. Wave after wave of pleasure flowed out to all her nerve endings. Her legs bowed as the final surge washed through her. Just as she came down from her high, her body relaxing, he let her legs drop to the bed. He leaned forward and began thrusting with quicker, less controlled strokes.

He didn't like to lose control. In bed however, she'd never had a problem getting him to let go. Now was no different. His face was positively feral as he crushed his mouth over hers. His tongue stroked her mouth as he reached his climax in one final thrust.

Panting, he collapsed on top of her, their slick bodies melding together. Sated, she traced her hand down the familiar lines of his back as he nuzzled her neck. Grinning, she finally gave a tiny push at his chest. "You're gonna kill me," she murmured.

Laughing, he rolled over and propped himself up on one elbow. A wide, satisfied grin spread across his face. "Still thinking about dating that cop?"

Her lips quirked up into a smile. "I never planned to. I just don't like you telling me what to do."

"Stubborn woman," he murmured, shifting over so he could discard the condom.

Groaning softly, she sat up and moved to the edge of the bed. Her feet hit the carpet and she dug her toes into the plush material as she stretched her legs out. She was a little sore but it had been worth it.

Like lightning, he reached out and snagged her by the waist, tugging her back against the mattress. Sage stared up at him as he once again covered her body.

"Where do you think you're going?" He pinned her to the bed, his legs encasing her thighs in an unrelenting embrace.

Her eyes widened when she realized he was hard again. It usually took him at least thirty minutes to recover. "You're..." She flicked her gaze down to his cock. From his half-sitting, half-laying position, it rested on her abdomen instead of teasing her pussy. She couldn't believe he'd already put on another condom. Apparently she'd underestimated him.

"Damn right I am. It's been over a year and a half since I've had this sweet pussy." He leaned down and gently touched his lips to hers, still making no attempt to shift down and slide into her.

He didn't actually say it but something in the way he said the words "a year and a half" told her he hadn't been with anyone since her. Even if he had, it wouldn't have mattered. Still, the thought jerked at her heartstrings in a way she hadn't thought possible.

This time there wasn't an urgency in his caresses. His tongue stroked hers as he reached between her legs and gently inserted two fingers. She tightened around him, savoring the feel of him teasing her.

Slowly, he dragged his fingers against her inner wall, drawing a moan of pleasure from her. When he pushed back in and rotated them, she squirmed.

She was already slick and perfectly stretched from their recent bout. Her body clenched around his thick fingers. She linked her hands through his hair, reveling in the fact that she was actually touching Trent again.

Even in her most ridiculous fantasies, she hadn't dared to hope she'd be able to touch or taste him again. A few stray tears escaped, spilling down her cheeks. Fate was either very kind, or seriously messing with her head. Either way, she wasn't going to balk at her second chance. However short she knew their time together would be. If someone was after her she couldn't drag Trent down with her.

Trent lifted his head and when their gazes met, his eyes searched hers for an answer. He must have tasted her tears so she was thankful when he didn't question her further.

Instead, he kissed her forehead, both cheeks, her nose, then her mouth again. Each kiss was done with such tenderness she could practically feel her heart swelling.

Damn it! He wasn't supposed to be like this. This was going to make it a thousand times harder if she had to walk away from him.

"I want you inside me," she whispered, almost hating to break the quiet moment but desperately needing that extra connection with him.

Wordlessly he withdrew his fingers and traced her clit in a sensual pattern. Shifting, he readjusted so he was cushioned between her legs, then buried his cock inside her.

She automatically arched her back at the intrusion. It seemed it didn't matter how often they had sex or how wet she was, her body always needed a moment to get used to his size.

"I've missed you, Sage." His words weren't a whisper. It was as if he was declaring it for the world to hear.

He held her gaze as he began to move inside her. Her throat tightened, barring her from saying she'd missed him too. The thought of admitting it out loud terrified her. The good things in her life were destined to be torn from her. She didn't want to lose Trent.

With his thumb he lazily traced the tip of her breast. When it was apparent she wasn't going to respond to his declaration, his head dipped and he raked his teeth over her other hardened bud. His tongue played an erotic dance, sending a chord of pleasure straight from her nipple to the pulsing between her legs.

It shouldn't be like this. Had never been like this with anyone before Trent. She didn't understand how he could bring so much pleasure to her body again so quickly after her toe-curling climax.

"Faster. Please." She didn't care that she was practically begging.

His hands moved to tighten around her hips, that firm grip so familiar. Her inner walls convulsed as he increased his speed. She could climax alone from the emotions echoing through her body.

Trent hungrily drove himself into Sage. His woman. He couldn't stop the possessiveness that threatened to overwhelm him just being near her, inside her. Even now, he was buried in her and he wanted more. More than just the physical connection.

She was holding back from him emotionally and he hated it. She didn't physically hold back though. No way in hell she could hide that kind of lust.

Those emotions poured off her in almost tangible waves. Every time she looked at him, he could feel her desire. The wanting. The need. Unfortunately, she kept everything else locked up tight.

That wasn't going to work. He wanted everything from her. And he planned to take it.

The tight walls of her slick sheath squeezed around him. His balls were pulled up painfully with the need for another release. But he restrained himself.

He gritted his teeth, holding back. Beneath him, Sage's body glistened with a light sheen of sweat. She was so close. Her contractions were coming quicker, a sure sign she was right there with him.

"Yesss," she hissed out. Her eyes were half closed and her hands dug into the sheet beneath her as she arched her back higher.

He cupped the perfect mounds she presented to him like an offering. Sucking one of her hardened buds, he teased the other, pinching and rotating it with little gentleness.

Almost immediately, her legs locked around his waist in a vise-like grip. She clawed at his back before her hands rested on his ass. She dug in hard, then shouted his name as the orgasm rushed through her.

That was all he needed to let go. Just hearing his name on her lips made him insane. With driving need, he rocked into her, jetting his semen into the condom, wishing it was directly inside her. His legs trembled with the force of his climax.

When he was sated, he stayed inside her a moment longer, his body fighting the withdrawal of her warmth.

"I wish we could stay like this forever," she mumbled so quietly he wondered if she was even aware she'd spoken.

Trent shifted and stretched out beside her. He placed a protective hand over her waist and pulled her close. When she smiled at him, his heart stuttered.

Actually stuttered. Like some love-sick fool.

After ten minutes, both their breathing had returned to normal. She pushed up and dropped a chaste kiss against his cheek. "I think I'm done for a while."

"We'll see about that." He playfully smacked her gorgeous ass as she slid from the bed.

CHAPTER FOUR

"Mind if I take a shower?" Trent grinned as she asked, but Sage shook her head knowingly. "*Alone.*" After everything that had happened in the past twenty four hours, she needed some serious alone time.

"Extra towels are in the linen closet." He followed suit and got out of bed, but moved toward his closet instead of the bathroom.

"Thanks," she murmured, watching the way his muscles flexed as he walked. Standing in the bathroom doorway, she paused, staring at him. She'd forgotten how sexy he looked naked. Okay, maybe she hadn't forgotten. More she'd forced herself to bury the memory.

Now she drank her fill of his long, muscular legs and wickedly broad back. She bit her lower lip as he bent over to pick something up. She sucked in a deep breath and her abdomen clenched. The man had the most perfect ass she'd ever seen. Definitely magazine worthy. She bit her bottom lip.

"Keep staring at me like that and it's time for round three." The laughter in his deep voice was unmistakable.

Embarrassed, she realized he was looking at her over his shoulder. She stepped inside the bathroom, shut the door and sagged against it. With everything going on it was wrong to even be with Trent right now. She didn't want to put him in any danger, but spending one night with him couldn't hurt. And for all she knew, the late night calls could be a prank. Although the break-in certainly wasn't. That was serious.

A shudder racked her body but she shook it off. She raked a hand through her tangled hair, then pulled out two towels from the cabinet. As she started to twist the shower knob, the door swung open.

"Ah, hey." Even though he'd just seen her naked, she held a towel against her chest.

The muscles in his neck corded tightly as his eyes roved over her barely covered body. Just like that heat flared inside her. She was close to dropping the towel and yanking him into the shower with her when he held out her cell phone.

"This was in your sweater pocket. It keeps ringing and I thought with everything that's happened it could be important."

"Thanks." Taking it, she held the towel against her chest as he shut the door behind him. She started to slide her finger across the screen to check her messages when it rang. Private number.

Not again.

All the muscles in her body pulled taut. She didn't want to answer. Not even a little bit. She worried if she ignored the caller she might piss off whoever was harassing her even more.

"Hello?"

"Hello, whore." This time it wasn't a mechanical voice but a man's. One she didn't recognize. Something vaguely familiar tickled at the far recesses of her brain but she couldn't have picked out the voice if her life depended on it.

"I'm getting tired of this. What do you want?"

"I think that much should be obvious."

Her legs grew weak so she leaned against the counter for support. "Well it's not." She barely squeezed the words out.

Anger laced his next words. "You're going to pay for tonight. I saw you tonight, putting yourself on display for anyone to see. Did you enjoy letting him fuck you up against your car?"

Rage washed over her but she jerked upright when she realized he hadn't stuck around. If he had, he would have known she and Trent hadn't had sex. Which meant he was probably the person who broke into her house. Maybe that was what had set him off, seeing her with Trent. Her hand fisted around the phone.

She started to hang up, not wanting to hear another word, when he continued. "I'm going to do to you what I did to your sister but first I'm going to kill your boyfriend."

She tried to push down the terror threatening to overwhelm her. "He doesn't mean anything to me! He's no one!"

"It doesn't matter. He dies too. Maybe this time I'll let you watch."

Before she could respond, he disconnected. Tears slipped down her face and she was powerless to stop them. The man who had raped and murdered her sister was behind bars. It couldn't be him calling. It just couldn't. Even if this was some sick prank, she had to warn Trent, then get as far away from him as possible.

No one was safe around her. And she wouldn't risk someone else dying because they had a connection to her.

CHAPTER FIVE

He didn't mean anything to her? Trent pushed away from the door. He hadn't heard the shower start so he'd gotten worried and wanted to check on her. Now he wished he hadn't. He grabbed her suitcases from downstairs and delivered them to the guestroom. If that's all she considered him—a good fuck—then she could go to hell.

He needed to get over her, get her out of his system for good. Something told him that might be damn near impossible though. After tossing her stuff in the other room, he found himself back in his room, pacing outside the bathroom door.

No matter that he told himself to walk away, his feet had a mind of their own. "Screw it," he mumbled to himself. They were going to have this thing out now. Opening the door, he slipped inside.

"Sage?" He saw her phone lying on the bathroom counter and his blood boiled. Just who had she been talking to anyway? An old boyfriend?

"Yeah?" The wobble in her voice made him pause.

"Are you okay?" Despite his anger, the sound of her upset primed all his protective instincts.

"I'm fine."

"We need to talk."

"Okay. Just give me a few minutes." The curt, broken answer was enough for him.

The hooks jingled against the rod as he yanked back the shower curtain. Sage stood under the streaming jet. When she heard the rustle, her eyes flew open and her hands quickly flew to cover her breasts—as if he hadn't just seen every inch of her naked, hadn't stroked her nipples until they were rock hard and desperate for his touch.

"What are you doing?" Her voice was shaky.

Her eyes were red and glassy and even though water flowed down her face and body, it was obvious she'd been crying. Instead of responding, he reached out and stroked her cheek with his thumb. And that was all it took. Her face crumpled and her hands fell away from her chest to cover her face. She twisted away from him but there wasn't anywhere to go in the shower.

"Aww, shit," he mumbled.

Crying women had never bothered him before. In his experience, women usually turned on the waterworks when they wanted something. That wasn't the case now. All his earlier anger slid away to be replaced by an overpowering desire to take on her pain.

He leaned over and twisted off the water, ignoring the spray of heat on his arm and upper body. "Come on, sweetheart." He guided her by the shoulders until she faced him.

Blindly she stumbled toward him, stepping over the small ledge. She wouldn't meet his gaze but her entire body shook as she buried her face in his chest. He wrapped his arms around her, holding on to her as she silently cried. For a woman she was fairly tall and he'd always thought of her as strong and lean, but naked and crying, she felt delicate and breakable.

His heart clenched as she shook against him. Whoever had upset her was going to pay. He stroked a soothing hand down her back until the trembling in her body slowly subsided. It didn't completely disappear though.

After a few minutes, she stepped away from him and wrapped her arms around herself. "I'm sorry. I'm such a mess," she mumbled and wiped at her eyes.

"Here." He grabbed one of the towels she'd laid out and wrapped it around her trembling shoulders.

He started to steer her to the door but she motioned toward the pool of water on the floor, then met his gaze. Her green eyes filled with more tears, ready to spill over again at the sight of the mess.

He couldn't help himself. A small chuckle escaped as he gently led her out of the room. "I don't give a shit about the water." All he cared about was getting her into bed.

Once outside the bathroom, she made a beeline for the bed and slipped under the covers after discarding her towel on the floor. Her eyes closed as her head hit the pillow and he knew her body was basically shutting itself down. He'd seen it happen too many times after battles. What she'd been through wasn't as strenuous of course but maybe she'd reached her limit.

"I'm so tired," she mumbled and rolled on her side, curling up with one of the pillows.

Too many things had happened to her today and her body needed rest. Someone had upset her though and pushed her over that edge. She'd been fine before going to take a shower, joking around even, but after that phone call, something had happened.

And he planned to find out what that something was.

Without shifting her too much, he lifted her head and positioned the discarded towel to soak up the water from her hair. He didn't want her to get sick on top of all this. He slid in behind her and held her close. "Who upset you?"

"I..." She paused for a moment and he wasn't sure she'd continue. "I don't know. It was a man and he threatened you. He said... he was going to kill you and make me watch. I think he saw us at the school. He made a comment about us fucking up against my car so he must not have stayed long enough to realize we didn't. It doesn't matter though, he wants to hurt you." Her voice broke on the last word and her body started to tremble.

Trent just held her tighter as he digested her words. The caller had to be connected to the break-in. No doubt about it in his mind. "Any idea who could be doing this?"

"No. I... no." She let out an angry curse, her body tense.

"We need to tell the police. They might be able to trace the call."

"It was a blocked number." Her voice was filled with resignation.

They still might be able to do more. "I'm going to call Steve tonight, let him know about the call."

"Okay, you're right. God, I'm so sorry about dragging you into this." Her voice cracked again so he turned her around and rubbed his hand up and down the length of her spine.

"Don't worry about me. I can take care of myself." And for damn sure he'd be taking care of her.

She wrapped her arms around him and buried her face against his chest as silent tears fell against him. Barely a few minutes later her breathing was no longer erratic but steady and rhythmic. She'd exhausted herself and now he hoped she'd get some actual rest.

Once he was sure she was sound asleep, he cleaned up the bathroom, checked all the doors and windows and double checked his security alarm for good measure.

Back in his room, he retrieved his cell phone and slipped out into the hall to call Steve. Once he'd updated the police about the most recent phone call Sage had received, he called his brother. Guilt washed over him that he hadn't called before now.

Jason picked up on the first ring. "Hey man, how is she?"

"I honestly don't know." He rubbed a hand over his stubbly face and leaned against the wall as he relayed everything that had happened right up until the mysterious late night phone call. Well, almost everything.

"Tell her to stay home tomorrow."

Trent snorted. "She won't listen."

"You're probably right. She's a stubborn ass woman."

There was no denying that. Sage was as stubborn as hell and they both knew that she'd be at work right after she made the official police report tomorrow morning.

"Fine, tell her to come in late then."

"No problem." He'd turned off the house phone and her cell so nothing would disturb her until she woke up on her own. Then she could take care of the police report and head to work. But he wanted her to get as much rest as she could. "Uh, listen...I need a favor. A big one."

"Okay."

"I want to have a friend of mine run her social security number, find out a little more about her past." What he was asking was pretty much illegal. Until he was officially a partner in his brother's construction company, he didn't have access to employee records and even if he did, he wasn't supposed to use them for his own purposes. It didn't matter if he wanted to help her or not. Trent hated putting his brother in this position but the police weren't going to put all their time and resources into her case. And he had much better and faster avenues to get answers.

Jason blew out a long breath. "I was afraid you might ask that."

"So is that a yes or a no?"

"You knew I'd say yes."

"I just want to help her."

"I know. I do too."

"Thanks, brother."

After they disconnected, he stripped off his shirt and as quietly as possible, slipped into bed. Sage was curled on her side so he moved in behind her and pulled her tight. She instinctively shifted closer. Whatever was going on in that head of hers, her body at least knew it was safe with him.

When she rubbed her backside over his already growing erection, he inwardly cursed. The sheet between them gave a basically non-existent barrier of separation and it did absolutely nothing to crush his ever-growing hunger for her.

Before meeting Sage, sex had been a very active part of his life. And wearing that Navy uniform had always gotten him plenty of ass. All he'd had to do was head to the nearest bar. Something he hadn't given much thought to before. He'd never been into long term commitments. Or any commitment really. One-night, or even two-night stands had been it for him.

Until he'd met her. Then he'd thrown everything he thought he knew about women out the window. Most of his friends weren't married but the few that were, seemed content to be with one woman. He'd never understood how that was possible until Sage.

Then he'd understood exactly why a man gave up being a bachelor.

It had nearly ripped his heart out when she'd decided to run out on him. In the middle of the night no less. He pushed the thought away and pulled her closer. She was with him now. That was what mattered.

Her ass moved again and his cock surged painfully. She wasn't waking up for a few hours at the very least and he certainly wasn't getting to sleep like this. Not when he was this wired. Sighing, he tried to relax against the pillow and inhaled her scent. It was something coconut, fresh and completely intoxicating.

Yeah, it was going to be a long night.

CHAPTER SIX

Sage opened her eyes and started to jerk upright but a heavy arm draped across her waist. For a moment, she almost panicked when she realized she was naked but the night before came rushing back with a vengeance. The vandalism, the phone call, and then her sobbing all over Trent.

She cringed when she remembered the way she'd lost it. She didn't understand why he even wanted her here with him anymore. She was such a mess. Moving slowly, she tried to slide off the bed when his hand clamped across her abdomen.

"Going somewhere?" Trent murmured. His low, seductive voice sent shivers throughout her entire body.

She tried to roll over but he kept her immobile. His erection pressed into her back, firm and insistent, but he seemed content to simply hold her. Despite the circumstances, she still felt secure with Trent, safe in his arms. She linked her fingers through his so that both their hands lay against her stomach.

"I've thought about you a lot the past couple years," she murmured into the quietness. She hoped she wasn't making a mistake by admitting it. She couldn't *not* tell him though.

It was still dark out but enough moonlight streamed in through the blinds. He had a masculine, wood sleigh bed, king-size of course. The dark blue comforter with pinched pleats was thick and warm, though not as warm as him. The man was a furnace, something she loved.

He was silent for a long moment and she wondered if he'd even respond. Her heart rate increased when he did. "I've thought about you too, probably too much... Is everything you told me about yourself true?"

Meaning back when they spent that intense week together. The hesitation in his voice clawed at her. She hated that he had to question her, even if she didn't blame him. She'd run like a coward because she'd been a complete wreck back then. He'd been the only bright spot in her life and she'd been too afraid to lean on him. She hadn't known him well enough and leaving had been easier. At least that was what she'd told herself.

"Yes. What I didn't tell you was that the night we met..." God, she still didn't know how to say the words. She wasn't ready to tell him what had happened to Marie; that she'd just come from her sister's murder trial the day they'd met. But Sage wanted to be more open with him. "It had just been a rough couple months," she finished lamely. "You and I met as I was leaving the city. I'd deleted all my social media accounts and was basically leaving everything behind. Or trying to."

"Did your leaving have to do with your sister?"

"Yeah," she rasped out.

His grip tightened around her. "I'm sorry." Even if he didn't know all of the truth, his words were sincere.

"I basically drove until I didn't trust myself to be on the road. I'd already sold almost everything I owned so it was easy to pick up and go. Then I met you having dinner at that bed and breakfast and I felt so guilty for having such an intense reaction to you." It had been like being hit with a bolt of lightning. Cliché but true.

"Guilty?"

"For being so attracted to you, for being happy around you." She didn't elaborate further and was glad when he didn't push.

He'd asked if he could join her for dinner since they'd both been eating alone, then afterward they'd shared a bottle of wine by the fire in that huge Victorian house turned B and B. They'd been the only patrons that first night and the owner had long since gone to bed. It had felt like they were the only two people in the world. When he'd asked if she wanted to join him in his room, the decision had been easy.

"What about your job and parents? Was that all true?"

"Everything I told you was the truth. Well, mostly. When I said I was taking time off from my job, I meant permanently. And, yes, my parents died years ago too. All that was true. So was where I went to college and all those silly family vacation stories I told you about."

Something inside him seemed to loosen at her words so she continued. "What about you? You were pretty vague about your parents." He'd told her about how his dad had died years ago in a construction accident, but he hadn't talked much about his mom. From Jason, Sage knew she was still alive.

Trent let out a breath, the warmth tickling the top of her head. "Not really sure where my mom is. Vegas maybe, last I heard anyway. Marriage and men are a fucking sport to her."

He didn't sound bitter, just resigned.

"That... sucks."

To her surprise, he let out a low chuckle. "It is what it is. She'll never change and I've stopped trying to think anything I or my brothers do will change her. Some holidays she'll show up on one of our doorsteps out of the blue, like months haven't passed since we last spoke. Sometimes she'll have someone with her, sometimes she'll be alone."

Sage turned in his arms, wanting to hold him closer. She'd had a pretty normal childhood. Her family had lived in a small town in upstate New York close to the Canadian border. Then just like all her high school friends she'd gone to college a few hours south. Moving to the city afterward had been a normal step for her.

It seemed like a lifetime ago. Since leaving she'd cut ties with almost everyone out of a sense of self-preservation. So many people had known her sister, it had just been too hard to stay in touch, to work at those relationships when she'd been hanging on by a thread.

"I'm sorry you guys aren't closer." She gently stroked a hand down Trent's back, enjoying the way his muscles tightened under her fingers. His erection was heavy between them, but he didn't seem to care. She was glad because this was nice.

Though that seemed like an inadequate word to describe the momentary peace she felt with him. They were sharing a pillow with no space between them and right now she had no desire to be anywhere else.

"I've got my brothers. And I have all my brothers from the Navy." The pride in his voice was evident.

He'd briefly told her that he'd been a SEAL, but other than that, he hadn't talked about it. "Do you miss the Navy?"

"Some days. It was time to get out though. I served my country but the overseas tours got exhausting. I always planned to move back here eventually, work with Jason. When he offered the partnership it was impossible to turn him down."

"Is your friend who's doing the security installation a former SEAL too?"

At that, Trent's lips curved up. "Yeah. I hope you'll get to meet him one day."

"Me too." And she meant it. She wanted to know everything about Trent's life. Even if she knew she shouldn't get too tangled up with him, it was hard not to. She'd fallen for him back at that bed and breakfast and she'd never gotten over him. She hadn't even slept with anyone since him.

"You like working in construction?" he asked after a few minutes of silence.

"I do. A lot actually. My degree is in business so I'm doing a lot of the same stuff I did before. But a lot of different stuff too. Your brother keeps me busy."

Trent snorted. "It's amazing he manages to check his damn email."

"God, right?" She scooted even closer to Trent, soaking up all his warmth. "I'm not complaining though. I've learned a lot the last six months. He takes me to all the job sites, lets me take part in pretty much anything I'm curious about. I like that every day is different. What about you?"

"I love working with my hands and yeah, I'm the same, I like that each day is different. For a while I contemplated going into law enforcement, but I knew it wasn't for me."

"Well, you *are* good with your hands," she murmured, sliding her hand lower until she gripped his backside with her fingers. His tight muscles flexed.

"Just good?" There was mock insult in his voice. His own hand trailed down her back, searching until he found exactly what he wanted.

She shrugged, fighting to keep a straight face. "Decent."

His fingers dug into her flesh as he brushed his lips over hers. "That sounds like a challenge."

"Maybe it is." She tightened her fingers even more.

"Hmm, I accept your challenge then." His voice was wicked and teasing as he slid his hand up her waist to one of her breasts and palmed it, rubbing in erotic little circles.

The pulse between her legs throbbed in tune with her heartbeat, completely wild and out of control. She clenched her legs together as he alternated between breasts. The man certainly knew how to bring her from zero to sixty in milliseconds.

When she reached between their bodies, ready to stroke him, he abandoned what he was doing to grip her arm and tug it back. She loved it when he took charge. Instead of returning to teasing her breasts, he trailed his hand down her back and spread her cheeks apart, tracing along her crease.

He watched her as he did, his expression intent. She started to tense when he feathered across her tight rosette. Just as quickly she relaxed when he playfully nipped her ear in that way he knew she loved.

Trent wouldn't hurt her or do anything she wasn't comfortable with.

She knew that on every level.

It was hard not to trust a man like Trent. He was still here with her even when he *knew* he could be in danger because of his connection to her. She didn't know what she'd done to deserve him and she wasn't sure she should stay. But the thought of walking away shredded her in ways she barely understood.

CHAPTER SEVEN

Sage pressed her intercom button. "Margo, I've got a few sets of plans I need sent overnight to the architect." Running on caffeine and nerves, she was glad that she was at least busy today. Neither Jason nor Trent had wanted her to come in today, but after stopping by the police station Trent had brought her straight here. There was simply too much to be done and if she'd stayed at Trent's place, she'd have gone stir crazy anyway. At least the police were looking into the phone calls now too, though she wasn't going to get her hopes up that they'd be able to find out who'd been calling her.

"No problem. I'll make sure they go out before I leave today. Also, there's someone holding on line one."

"Who is it?"

"A man named Anthony Deal but he wouldn't tell me who he was with. Want me to send him to voicemail?"

"No!" She cleared her throat. "Uh, no I'll take it." She'd been waiting on this call. Anthony Deal, District Attorney in New York, was a hard man to get a hold of but he always went out of his way to be kind to her.

She picked up the line immediately. "Sage here."

"Sage, I received your message. Is everything all right?"

She nervously smoothed a hand over her skirt, drying her suddenly damp palm. "I don't know anymore."

"Well, Max Lucero is still in jail so rest easy."

She knew that. He'd told her the same thing a couple of weeks ago when she'd called. "That's not why I'm calling. I told you about the weird calls but last night someone broke into my place and wrote a disturbing message on my wall and a picture frame of me and... Marie. Then I received another phone call that was really disturbing. The caller said..." She cleared her throat, trying to push the words out. "He said he was going to do to me what he did to my sister. But Lucero's still in jail so I don't know what's going on."

Silence greeted her ears.

"Anthony?"

"Shit," he muttered.

Icy panic slithered down her spine. "What is it?"

"I guess it could be a prank but...damn it Sage, I'm sorry to tell you like this."

"Tell me what?" The vise around her heart twisted tighter.

"They found two semen specimens at the scene but there wasn't enough to identify the other one and it was older than Lucero's."

"What?" Her knees gave out on her as she collapsed in her chair.

"It had been in her system about twelve hours before Lucero. For all we know, it was from a date the night before."

"What the hell are you talking about? Why wasn't this covered at the trial?" Now she was shouting. Her sister had been held captive for a day and a half and even she knew time stamping DNA wasn't an exact science. What if they'd gotten the time line wrong? The police had decided that her sister had been taken in the early morning hours but Sage hadn't come home from work the night before so for all they knew, she'd been taken the previous night. No one had wanted to listen to her though.

Margo popped her head in, worry plain on her face but Sage waved her away.

"We had it suppressed. All the evidence pointed to Lucero. He practically confessed and he never mentioned an accomplice. It was a slam dunk."

"And you didn't think it necessary to tell *me* any of this?" Her heart beat an erratic rhythm against her ribcage. If she'd known all this, she'd have done more about the late night calls.

"I wanted to wait until after the trial but then you disappeared."

That was a pathetic excuse. The man who'd killed her sister had done it to get to her. He'd admitted it. "I can't believe you!"

"I'm going to contact the local police and brief them on your situation. You'll have security twenty-four hours a day. I'm also going to send a team to interview Lucero, see if we can get something more out of him."

"And why didn't you do this two years ago?" she snapped.

"We didn't think it was relevant." He sighed.

"Why not?"

"Your sister was…"

"What?" she demanded.

"You know what kind of lifestyle she led. We just assumed it was from one of her lovers. We didn't think it was relevant...and we didn't want to prejudice the jury."

She noticed he kept using the word "we". Whenever he put the blame on other people, he used we but when he won a case, he used "I". What a bastard. She couldn't believe she'd ever put her faith in the man.

Her fingers tightened around the phone. "So she liked to date and party. Big deal. What twenty-something girl doesn't? You should have dug deeper. At the very least, you should have told me about it. I've been walking around thinking this was some fluke because that bastard's in jail. Until the break-in and phone call last night I wasn't even truly worried. You're lucky I'm not dead!" *Or worse.* She clutched the phone tighter against her ear, wishing it was his neck. Just because her sister had loved to party didn't mean she'd deserved what happened to her.

No one deserved to be raped and strangled to death. Especially not someone as carefree and full of life as Marie had been. And now it looked like some lunatic actually was after Sage.

"I'm sorry Sage. That's all I can give you right now. If Lucero did have an accomplice, we'll find him. I promise."

"Go to hell." She slammed the phone into the receiver. Her body shook with rage and a healthy dose of fear. How had this person found her? She'd started using her mother's maiden name, moved hundreds of miles away and worked at a mid-sized construction company as opposed to a multi-million dollar magazine enterprise.

She glanced at her wall clock. It was almost three. "Thank God," she muttered under her breath. Despite all her inner turmoil, the day had flown by quickly. At least that was one thing to be grateful for. She chewed on the end of her pen. Now she was actually glad Trent had insisted on purchasing her a security system. And she was going to pay him back. For how she felt, he could argue all he wanted, it didn't matter. She was taking back control of her life.

Trent had been amazing last night and this morning. She might have warned him about the threatening caller, but tonight she had to tell him everything that had happened to her sister. She wouldn't blame him if he decided she was too much trouble after he learned everything about her past. She couldn't let anything happen to Trent. He was much too special to her and the longer she was around him, the more attached she got.

After a few minutes of deep breathing, she swiveled around from her desk to her work station and spread out her notes. It was time to focus on work. She had to update both her calendars if she wanted to keep Jason squared away. So much was happening so fast with the company it was only a matter of time before they needed to hire a couple more people. And if she could focus on work, maybe she could forget the other bullshit for a couple hours.

The next time she glanced at her clock, an hour had passed. Most of her anger had dissipated but the fear still lurked at the surface.

The door to her office opened but she didn't bother turning around. "The outgoing plans are rubber banded Margo." The other woman was sweet and Sage didn't want her seeing her upset. Margo would inevitably ask questions and right now she didn't have any answers.

A heavy hand came down on her shoulder and she nearly jumped out of her skin until she realized who it was. "Hey, what are you doing here?"

Trent was supposed to have been at a job site. She couldn't handle seeing him now, not when she felt so weak and vulnerable.

Trent rotated her chair so that she faced him. Then he placed both hands on the armrests, caging her in. "I came by to drop off some paperwork for Jason." His voice was low, deep, intoxicating.

"He's not here," she breathed out, hating the inviting tone of her voice and hating the way her body was turned on at the mere sight of him. It was like a switch inside her flipped when he came around.

He grinned wickedly as he leaned closer, raking his teeth against her jaw. "I know."

She shivered at the sensation. "Trent..."

He brushed his mouth over hers, his tongue probing, teasing, taking. As he deepened the kiss, he slid a hand up her leg and under her skirt. When he toyed with the edge of her panties rapid heat pooled between her legs. They couldn't do this here though, not with Margo in the next room. Before she could say anything, her office door opened. Margo stood in the doorway, blinking in surprise.

"The plans are over there." Trent nodded toward one of the tables as he slid his hand down but not completely away from her leg. He seemed completely unfazed at being caught like this.

Too mortified to speak, Sage shoved at his hand. His eyes danced with barely contained amusement but at least he stood and had the decency to step back.

The other woman averted her gaze, grabbed what she needed and shuffled toward the door.

"Margo?" Trent spoke.

"Yes?" She wouldn't meet his gaze.

Sage wished the floor would open and swallow her whole. She tried to think of something to say for damage control, but at this point she didn't think there was much she *could* say.

"As soon as those go out you can lock up and leave." Trent's words were a command.

Margo shut the door behind her without a response, though Sage was fairly positive she heard muted laughter from the other office.

Sage immediately stood. "Damn it, Trent, now she's going to think—"

He advanced, pushing her against the desk. He attempted to silence her with another kiss but she pressed a hand to chest, forcing him back. "No."

Groaning, he lifted his head. "What is it woman? I've had a hard-on all day thinking about you." As if he needed to show her, his hips surged forward, grinding against her. Then, as though he thought she didn't get the hint, he grabbed the hand she'd placed on his chest and moved it to his cock.

"Feel that?"

"Yes...no, damn it, stop for one second. We need to talk." She wrenched her hand away and he sighed in frustration.

"Can it wait until tonight?" He traced a finger down her cheek and jaw bone and settled deeper up against her, spreading her legs apart with his thigh.

"It's important."

"Are you married or dating someone?" His finger delved lower, to her collarbone, playing with the edge of her blouse. Her breasts immediately grew heavy with need.

"You know I'm not," she breathed out.

"Are you planning to quit here?"

She shook her head.

"Then it can wait until later."

No. The voice in her head screamed to stop but that noisy bitch was silenced when he nipped her jaw. God, she was weak. It was as if she was possessed whenever she was around him. Part of her wanted one last time with him before she told him the truth about her past. Because if he decided she was too much trouble, she'd have one more memory of him to keep. Oh yeah, weak and greedy for him.

"Fine," she breathed out. She *would* tell him over dinner. Inwardly she cursed her own weakness but rationalized another hour or two with him wouldn't affect anything.

In the distance she was vaguely aware of the bell attached to the front door dinging. She had no doubt Margo would lock up like she always did. They were alone now.

"She's gone," Trent murmured before claiming her mouth in such a possessive, demanding way she had no choice but to grab onto him for support.

She clutched at his shoulders and when he moved to nuzzle her neck, she let out a low moan. He raked his teeth over her sensitive skin, drawing another gasp from her. They were at work, something she'd had general fantasies about in the past but nothing compared to the reality.

"I want to fuck you long and hard over this desk. When you come, I want my name on your lips." His words sounded ragged and almost forced, as if he found it difficult to even speak.

Her inner walls spasmed. He'd never been a big talker during foreplay and though his words weren't particularly dirty, they lit the match on her desire.

When his hand made its way back up her skirt, she thought she'd come the moment he touched her. He had that much power over her.

Pushing her panties away, he rubbed a thumb over her sensitive clit, drawing a moan from somewhere deep inside. She'd worn a looser skirt today but hadn't imagined they'd be doing this on her work desk.

Trent made her feel things she'd never thought possible. When she was with him, everything felt right, as if they could have something real. If only her past hadn't come back to haunt her.

"Stop thinking," he murmured against her neck.

"What?"

"Your entire body is tense. Relax and focus on the present." His low spoken words were a soft demand.

Forcing herself to focus on his hands and mouth, she eased back until she was perching on the edge of the desk. One finger, then two delved inside her slit while his thumb continued the onslaught against her clit. She worked her hips against his hand.

When he increased his momentum, she blindly reached out and started working at his belt buckle, tugging until the blasted thing came free. If he was going to tease her, she wanted to tease him right back.

He shifted to give her better access. Without hesitation she slipped her hand under his jeans, pushing them down. She felt his cock spring free and sighed in appreciation. He was thick, long and absolute perfection. She wrapped her hand around his erection and began slowly stroking him as she cupped his balls. He shuddered, groaning at her caresses.

Trent jerked under Sage's erotic touch. He could feel himself close to the edge but he didn't want to come in her hands. Though his body fought it, he pulled away from her for a second.

She started to protest until he snagged a condom out of his pocket before shucking his pants and T-shirt. As he quickly rolled it on, he felt like a randy teenager again. In a few seconds he had her skirt and top pooled on the floor with his clothes. She'd worn another one of those button-up type shirts and he was thankful they seemed to be her normal work attire. Easier access for him.

His hands shook—actually shook—when he'd drawn her top open this time. Somehow he managed not to rip the buttons free. The only thing stopping him from acting like a total animal was the fact that they'd have to go out in public after this.

Just as quickly, he tossed her bra to the side. The need to see her completely bare drove him crazy.

Emotionally, she seemed determined to keep him at arm's length and after all the stuff he'd discovered today, he thought he knew why. Not that he gave two shits about that. If she thought she could scare him off, she was wrong. He was going to be in her life and it was about damn time she got used to it.

She'd run from him once and even though he might have an understanding why, it wasn't happening again. She was his.

The more sex they had, the more he was claiming her. He wondered if she understood that he'd do any damn thing for her.

Now she stood in front of him wearing a simple black thong and three-inch fuck-me heels. His balls pulled up so tight he was ready to slide right into her and find that ultimate release. When she raked her nails down his chest, he almost did just that but somehow he restrained himself.

"Lay back." It wasn't a request.

Her cheeks flushed pink but she did as he said, shoving papers and file folders out of the way. Her back arched as she spread herself out like a sacrifice for him.

Staring at her, he had to remind himself to breathe. He traced his finger along her opening and smiled when she jumped. Her sweet scent rolled over him as her leg muscles tightened and her hips shifted, scooting closer to the edge of the desk. Oh yeah, she wanted this as bad as he did.

He thought about teasing her a little longer but when she moaned he buried his tongue deep inside her. She tasted sweet and if the mewling sounds she kept making were any indication, it wouldn't take her long at all. He groaned against her slick folds, savoring all of her.

Moving his tongue in and out of her warmth he took pure satisfaction from the small, jerky motions she made each time he stroked her. Oh yeah, he was claiming her, something she had to know on a subconscious level.

Shifting her body, he pulled her closer to the edge of the desk so he could taste more. With a long swipe, he started as far back as she'd allow him and licked from her tight rosette back up to her pulsing clit. He flicked across her sensitive bundle of nerves, earning another yelp from her.

God, she was perfection.

Her legs trembled almost violently so he placed a strong hand on her inner thigh when she started to crush his head. When he chanced looking up at her, her eyes were closed but she was touching herself. Rubbing over her breasts and stomach.

He loved that she was so relaxed and free with him, at least when they were like this. There weren't any barriers between them. After this he wanted to break all of them down. No more secrets. Last night when they'd talked and held each other he'd felt as if she'd started to open up to him again, but she was still afraid, still worried.

He increased his tempo against her clit and inserted two fingers. Her inner muscles clenched as a rush of cream soaked his fingers and when she started climaxing, he stood and joined with her, pushing balls deep.

Her eyes were glazed over as she rode through the last waves of her orgasm. And he wasn't far behind her. Gripping her hips, he thrust forward as she clenched around him. The suctioning sound of his cock moving in and out of her was the only noise in the quiet office.

Every time she was in here, he wanted her to think of this, of him.

His abdominal and thigh muscles clenched as he emptied himself into the condom. When the unbidden fantasy of being inside her with no barrier played in his mind for the second time in twenty-four hours, he groaned and thrust one last time before falling onto the desk. With his hands, he braced himself on either side of her head, staring down at her. The slender legs around his waist shifted when he moved but she kept her ankles secure behind him.

Fine with him, he didn't want to go anywhere either.

A satisfied smile played on her lips. "I can't believe we just did that," she murmured.

"Are you on the pill?" he blurted.

Still breathing hard, she shook her head.

"We'll set up an appointment or do whatever you need to do."

She simply nodded, but something in her gaze bothered him. No fucking way. He couldn't deal with any more barriers. Not anymore. Looked like it was time to have that talk.

Slowly he eased out of her, his dick protesting the entire time. Inside Sage was exactly where he wanted to be.

After they were both dressed she avoided his gaze and started shutting the computer down. It was as if she was physically erecting those damn walls between them again and it pissed him off.

"I know your last name is—was—Radford." The words were out before he could stop himself or second guess the decision to tell her what he'd discovered today.

She was slightly bent over, her hand on her mouse, but her spine straightened at his words. Which was sort of the effect he'd been going for. He was sick of her half-truths. Maybe taking her off guard was the only way she'd be straight with him.

Sage swiveled as she stood and almost lost her footing. He made a move to help her but she backed away. "What the hell did you just say?"

"I know your last name was Radford before you changed it to Miller."

"Get out of here," she snapped.

"What?"

Completely taking him by surprise, she charged at him. She pushed her finger against his chest until he was in the outer lobby. "Get the hell out of here," she ground out.

He'd never seen her so angry before and wasn't quite sure what he'd done to warrant it. She was the one who'd been lying to him. Not the other way around. "Sage—"

"Now." She turned on her heel and slammed the door to her office.

He sighed and rubbed a hand over his face when he heard the lock slide into place.

"Fucking women," he muttered.

CHAPTER EIGHT

S age re-buttoned her blouse when she realized she'd missed two the first time, but her hands wouldn't stop shaking. She knew she shouldn't have shouted at him like that, but he'd taken her so off guard she'd simply reacted out of fear.

She had no idea how or when he'd learned her real last name, but he'd obviously done a little investigation. After setting the phones to voicemail mode, she grabbed her purse and readjusted her skirt.

She'd had enough of manhandling and people invading her privacy to last a lifetime and while she couldn't exactly blame him, the last thing in the world she'd expected was for Trent to do the same thing. She hadn't heard the door alarm go off so she knew he was still out there.

Well, she couldn't hide in her office forever. Taking a deep breath, she opened her door and sure enough, there he was leaning against Margo's desk. With his big arms crossed over his chest, his expression dark, a little shiver went down her spine. "I'm sorry I kicked you out of my office."

"Why did you?"

"You took me off guard and I panicked."

He watched her for a long moment before tilting his head toward the door. "Come on, let's get out of here. We'll talk in the truck."

Being in an enclosed space with him when she could still smell him on her probably wasn't the best idea if she wanted to think clearly, but he'd insisted on driving her to work that morning instead of taking her to her place to let her pick up her car. Without responding, she fished her keys out of her purse and walked out the front door. Silently, he followed and waited until she'd locked up. She kept stride with him as they walked down a couple blocks to where he was parked. Out of the corner of her eye, she saw him looking around, scanning the quiet commercial block. She was looking for anyone watching her too and appreciated how vigilant he was, even while she hated that he had to be careful in the first place.

Not that she expected less from him. But she didn't want to be responsibility, a weight around his neck.

When he opened the passenger door for her, she shouldn't have been surprised, but the gesture still touched her.

Once he'd gotten in and started the ignition, her tension only ratcheted up.

"The alarm system I was telling you about is being installed today," he said before she could speak.

"You can take me home if you want." It would be the smart thing for him to do and she wanted to give him an out.

"You're out of your pretty little mind, sweetheart. They won't be finished until later tonight anyway." He glanced over his shoulder as he pulled out into traffic, heading straight out of town.

"Supposedly the alarm system is the best, right?"

"Yep." His jaw twitched but he didn't look at her.

"Then why won't you take me home and I'll wait until it's ready?"

"Not until I do a few test runs. If everything is satisfactory, you can move back tomorrow." *And I'll be staying with you.*

He didn't voice the last part but she could practically hear the words roll off his tongue.

"Trent, someone is *stalking* me. Someone dangerous. He knows about you and threatened you last night. I appreciate everything you're doing, but maybe… you need to stay away from me."

A bark of laughter rumbled deep in his chest, but there was no amusement in the sound.

"If you know my real last name, then you know all about what happened to my sister. The longer you're around me, the more danger you're putting yourself in. That was what I wanted to tell you…before," she finished lamely. She could feel heat creeping up her neck, wishing she hadn't started that thought.

His cell phone rang and he actually answered, completely ignoring her pleas. She wanted to scream in frustration.

"Yeah, I've got her with me right now…okay…okay…I'll contact you if anything comes up but we'll be staying at my place tonight…yep, they'll be finished with the installation by tomorrow."

"Who was that?" she asked the second he hung up.

"Steve." He shot her a sideways glance, annoying her even more when he didn't elaborate.

"Will you please tell me what's going on?"

He lifted a shoulder as he pulled into his driveway. "Wait until we get inside the house."

The way he ordered her got her back up straight, but he was out of the truck and moving to the front door before she could respond. Frustrated, she jumped down from the truck and stalked behind him.

* * *

Stupid, fucking bitch.

She was making him crazy. He slapped his cheeks a few times, trying to keep awake as he waited for Sage to leave work. He hadn't been to sleep in… he couldn't remember how long. Since he'd arrived in Hudson Bay. It was all Sage's fault. He couldn't even get off to pictures of her anymore.

Because he needed her. Nothing else would do.

When he saw her step from her place of employment, he automatically shifted forward in the driver's seat. But he stiffened as that hulking guy strode out with her. The man scanned the street, his gaze vigilant. It scanned over his car, didn't linger too long.

His car had tinted windows so he wasn't worried about being recognized but he crouched down a little lower anyway. His heart raced as he watched them get into the guy's truck. Sage's car was still outside her town home downtown.

He knew because he'd driven by a couple times today. It hadn't moved. So she'd definitely gotten a ride from someone to work; probably the man she was leaving with now.

He certainly hoped so since he'd planted something special on the undercarriage of the guy's truck. Small and nearly undetectable unless you knew what you were looking for.

As the truck pulled away from the curb, Sage inside it, he forced himself to remain still. He wouldn't follow her now. He had too much to do before he made his move against her, made her his forever.

He took a sip of his tepid coffee before grabbing his tablet from the passenger seat. He ran his finger over it, waking it from sleep mode. When he tapped on the app he was using to follow the tracker he'd planted, his heart rate kicked up a notch.

It was working.

He could see the little red dot moving down the street, then turning, heading out of town. Yep, she definitely wasn't going home.

Which meant he wouldn't bother heading that way either. He had too much to do anyway. Starting the engine, he grinned to himself as he pulled onto the road. It was time to pick up a few supplies. He'd already brought some with him, but he needed to be prepared for a worst case scenario.

No way would he go to jail so he had to have a foolproof plan in place in case things went south.

If he couldn't have Sage no one could. He was willing to die for her. He doubted that fucker driving her around cared about her that much.

That was what was so wrong with her, with all women. They always picked the wrong men. They didn't care about the nice guys, the ones who were right in front of them, willing to listen and give up valuable time.

Fucking women always went for the wrong men. Just like Sage. She'd chosen wrong and soon he'd make her see just how badly she'd screwed up.

On the way to the hardware store, his blood sang in his veins, readying for what was to come.

Soon he'd feel Sage's tight body up against his, around his cock, while he pounded into her. He'd hurt her like he'd hurt her sister, make her watch the video he'd made.

In the end nothing could save her. Because they were going to be together forever.

He just had to make sure everything was ready for that final step.

CHAPTER NINE

As soon as they stepped through the front door, Sage started firing questions at Trent.

"Damn it woman, let me reset the alarm."

When he flipped open the key pad cover next to the hall closet, she continued down the hallway to the kitchen. If there was ever an excuse to drink, today was it. Even though she was anything but relaxed, she smiled when she found a six pack of light beer in the refrigerator.

"Will you grab one for me too?"

She glanced over her shoulder as Trent entered the room. "Depends. You ready to give me some answers?"

"I was ready at the office, until you decided to have a tantrum."

"A tantrum?"

He took the beer she handed to him and leaned against one of the granite countertops. His kitchen was sleek and modern, with stainless steel and all the newest appliances. "What would you call it?"

She fought the urge to wipe the smirk off his face, mainly because he wasn't wrong. "Look, I don't want to argue. Can you please tell me how you know my real last name?"

"I had a friend run your social security number and even then it wasn't easy but combined with what you'd already told me about your sister, it wasn't too hard to figure out who you are."

She gnawed on her bottom lip. Well that certainly didn't make her feel better. It hadn't taken Trent long at all.

"Do you finally feel like telling me everything you've been holding back?"

"You obviously know what happened to my sister?" At his nod, she continued. She was grateful she didn't have to tell him all the details. "I didn't tell you last night but... the day we met is the day my sister's killer was convicted. I left right after the trial. There's no way to say it other than I was really messed up when I met you, Trent. I hadn't been able to grieve until I knew that bastard was going to pay for what he did. Then I met you at that silly little bed and breakfast and you made me feel alive." Had he ever. He'd been so open, so giving. He still was. It killed her to think something could happen to him because of her.

"So why'd you leave then?" His expression was completely neutral.

She ached to cross over to him and pull him into her arms, but wasn't sure if he'd accept her embrace now. "I meant it last night when I said I felt guilty, being so happy with you. But mainly, I needed to start over somewhere. Start fresh. I'd only planned to stay there a night...then you came along and..." She shrugged.

He set his beer down and stalked toward her. Immediately she tensed, ready for his rejection, but when he wrapped his arms around her and pulled her close she melted into him. Even if she hated reliving the darkest time of her life, a small part of her felt liberated that she could finally admit to him what had happened.

"I'm truly sorry about your sister," he murmured into her hair. His deep voice reverberated through her veins, soothing every part of her.

Not trusting her voice, she nodded into his chest. She'd done enough crying already to last a lifetime. After a few moments, she took a small step back. "There's more."

"I think I know what you're going to say. I stopped by the Sheriff's Department to check on your case right before I came to see you at work.

Steve had just received a call from a very agitated District Attorney in New York with instructions to protect you. I told him what I'd found out and he filled me in as best he could."

"That was fast."

"You better believe it. They've got two undercover guys watching your place in case your stalker makes a move and later tonight they're sending someone to stake out my place."

"Really?" Anthony had told her he'd take care of it but after the way he'd lied to her before she hadn't been so sure she could depend on him.

"The DA knows he fucked up and from the way Steve told it, the guy wants to keep you safe. Why are you surprised?"

"I'm not. I guess this all feels surreal, to be dealing with this again." She grabbed her drink and went to sit at the kitchen table. Her legs felt as if they might give way at any moment. Stuff like this wasn't supposed to happen *twice* in a lifetime. She'd finally started to move on.

Trent sat across from her, refusing to give her space. Apparently he knew her better than she knew herself. "For the record, you're not leaving my side until we figure out who's been stalking you."

She clasped her hands around the cold beer, the feel of it against her fingertips as icy as the chill of fear raking through her. He shouldn't be around her. Hell, he shouldn't *want* to be around her. "Listen, I agree that I need protection but don't you think it's smarter if I have someone less involved stay with me? You might as well paint a big target on your forehead. This guy already knows that we're—"

"It's not up for discussion. Someone will be with you at all times, including at work. I'm not taking chances with your safety and I'm not walking away from you. Deal with it."

God, she wanted to cry again as she looked at him. Throat tight, she simply nodded because she didn't trust her voice, not with the surge of emotion pummeling through her.

Thankfully he continued. "Jason knows everything too now, and he's going to handle telling Margo."

Sage hadn't even thought about that, but she should have. She'd been so wrapped up in her own fear. Even if Trent had found out who she was, she wanted to tell him some of the details about her past so he heard them from her, not some report.

"Lucero was obsessed with me." She swallowed hard, was grateful when he simply took her hands in his. It made it easier.

"He was a photographer right?" he gently prodded.

She nodded. "At *En Vogue*, where I worked. He was actually an assistant photographer and it was like overnight he developed this weird obsession with me. They finally fired him and even then I had to take out a restraining order." It had been a nightmare. The man had shown up everywhere she went. At parties, clubs, even her damn gym. She'd moved twice and changed her number at least five times but it didn't matter. Somehow, he'd always tracked her down.

"Do you think he was working with someone?"

She understood the question because it wasn't a coincidence that she was being stalked and threatened now. "He never hinted about having a partner. If he did, I don't understand how the police missed it."

"Maybe it was someone who took an interest in the case or in you. Or in him."

She nodded. It could be any of those things, or he could have had a partner. None of the options really mattered. What did matter was that someone was stalking her now and wanted to hurt Trent. She couldn't let that happen. "Look, if you... if you wanted to walk away or let me stay at my own place I'd understand. I know I'm bringing a lot to the table and I don't want you to feel obligated to protect me."

Trent's fingers tightened around hers before he abruptly stood and headed for the refrigerator. "You hungry?"

She nearly got whiplash from the change in topic. "Don't you want to talk about this?" She'd given him an out and part of her wished he'd take it. The selfish part didn't want him to because she couldn't bear to walk away from him herself.

"What's there to talk about? Someone wants to kill you and I'm not going to let it happen. I'll worry about you and let the cops worry about him. And if you think I'd just leave you alone during all this, you don't know me at all." His neck muscles were corded tightly as he moved around the kitchen, every line in his body pulled taut with a simmering anger.

It wasn't that she didn't know him, it was that she didn't want him to get hurt. How could he not see that? She didn't have the energy for an argument though. "I'm going to take a quick nap before dinner. Is that okay or do you need my help?"

Still not looking at her, he spoke, his words curt. "I'll wake you in an hour."

She wanted to reach out to him, to touch him, but it was clear he needed space. And she was afraid that she'd break down crying if he rejected her so she left the room.

* * *

Trent pulled out a rectangular pan and slammed it down on the counter a little too hard before greasing it. Did Sage really not know how he felt about her? Hell, even if he didn't love her he'd be staying with her, protecting her. How could he not? He didn't know what kind of men she was used to but her perception of the opposite sex was about to undergo major surgery.

After combining all the ingredients, he set the timer to forty-five minutes and slid the chicken vegetable casserole into the oven. He started to go join Sage and catch a few minutes of rest but stopped when his phone buzzed against his hip.

When he saw Steve's name on the caller ID he answered. "Yeah?"

"Everyone is in place. So far there's been no unusual activity at Sage's."

He walked down the hall to his living room and peered through the blinds. Sure enough, a car sat across the street. "I see your guy."

"Good. I'll probably make a drive by later. Can Sage talk right now?"

"She's taking a nap."

"When she wakes up ask her about a man named Graham Hartigan. He was the head photographer at *En Vogue* and worked closely with Lucero."

"So?"

"I just got a call from New York and Lucero's now claiming Hartigan was his partner."

"And they don't believe him?"

"The DA thinks he might say anything to get moved."

"Moved?"

"Yeah, he wants to move from Cell Block A to C. Apparently he doesn't like being the bitch to a bunch of neo-Nazis." Steve grunted.

"Have they cut him a deal?"

"If his story checks out they will. Everything okay on your end?"

"She's taking everything as well as can be considered." She would pull through this, he had no doubt.

"All right. I'll call you with any updates."

After they disconnected he hurried up the stairs. In the middle of his bed, Sage lay curled on her side clutching a pillow. He hadn't gotten much sleep the night before but he knew if he joined her now, he wouldn't get any either. His cock lengthened painfully as he watched her.

With her face relaxed, she actually looked peaceful. The desire to feel her naked body against his and admit how much she meant to him nearly overwhelmed him but he shut the door and left her alone instead.

CHAPTER TEN

S age opened her eyes to a gentle hand on her shoulder. "Has it been an hour already?"

Trent nodded, his lips pulled up into a slight smile. "Afraid so. You want me to hold dinner for you?"

Stretching her arms above her head, she shook her head. "No, if I don't get up now, I'll wake up at three this morning and won't be able to go back to sleep." Her body screamed to stay under the warm covers but she forced her legs to obey and get out of bed.

He'd turned the heater on high but her yoga pants and matching tank top didn't help the chill that had descended on her so she threw on the sweatshirt she'd discarded earlier.

A small frown marred Trent's face as they walked toward the door.

"What?"

His frown turned to a mischievous grin, making her belly flip-flop. "I can't see your nipples through that thing."

"Pervert." Half-smiling, she nudged him with her hip. Her stomach was growling and if she let him, they'd end up in his bed before she got some sustenance.

"Steve called while you were sleeping and wanted to talk to you about a Graham Hartigan."

She nodded at the familiar name. "He was one of the top photographers where I used to work."

"Lucero claims he was his partner."

She stumbled on the bottom stair but Trent steadied her. "What?"

"They don't know if he was actually involved or if Lucero's lying to get a transfer."

She was silent as she digested the information and when Trent pulled out a chair for her, she gratefully sat at the round kitchen table. She traced her finger over the solid wood. "He did ask me out a few times but he was harmless." Or she'd assumed he was.

Trent placed a plate in front of her. "Eat."

Nodding, she took a bite. She felt too nauseous to eat but forced herself to chew and swallow. After she'd eaten a little more, Trent spoke again. "What else do you remember about him?"

"Not much except that he used more product in his hair than most women I know." *He couldn't have been involved, could he?* It just didn't seem feasible.

"How did he take it when you turned him down?"

"Okay I guess. The first time he obviously didn't get the hint but the second time he actually asked me out in front of other people so I was pretty firm. He didn't bother me after that. In fact, he kind of avoided me." The second time he'd asked her for a date had been at the company Christmas party. She'd felt a little bad at embarrassing him in front of people but she'd also been pissed that he'd tried asking her out in front of others. Maybe he'd hoped she'd say yes since they weren't alone.

Trent started to speak when his phone buzzed. He glanced at the caller ID. "It's Steve," he said to her before swiping his finger across the screen.

Sage pushed her chicken around her plate while they talked. All Trent's answers were one word. Curt and to the point. Whatever was going on, she knew it wasn't good.

As soon as he disconnected, set her fork down. "What did he say? Good news? Bad news?"

He rubbed a hand over his face and pushed his plate away. "Both. The good news is it looks like Hartigan was Lucero's partner."

What little food she'd eaten rolled around in her stomach. The sick freak should be rotting in jail. Not free, enjoying his life after he'd raped and killed her sister. "Why is that a good thing?"

"At least we know who we're after now. He's not some faceless target we're looking for anymore."

"Okay, what's the bad news?"

"He's gone missing."

"Missing?" She pressed a hand to her stomach, afraid she might be sick.

"He hasn't shown up for the last few photo shoots he was scheduled for and when they sent a couple officers down to question him about his involvement with Lucero, he was gone. And... He had a virtual shrine set up to you at his apartment."

"What?" All the air left her lungs in one whoosh.

Trent nodded, his expression grim.

She wanted to panic, but shoved all those emotions back down. Now wasn't the time for that. "Then why did he wait so long to come after me?"

"You moved here what, six months ago?" At her nod, he continued. "What were you doing the year before that?"

"Traveling. My sister and I always talked about taking a road trip, so after...after everything, I did all the things we'd ever wanted to."

"It sounds like you were never in one place long enough for him to track you. Contrary to popular belief, unless you're with the government or you're a hacker, it's not easy to track someone's credit card movements without shelling out a boatload of cash. My guess is he sporadically ran checks on your social security number, maybe he had a friend helping, who knows but he probably got a hit here not too long ago."

"So why not just come after me? Why all the stupid calls?"

"According to Steve he's been in Australia the past month working on a contracted shoot. And, he might want you but he hates you, which means he wants to make you suffer. He probably got off thinking he was terrifying you."

"And now he wants to kill me." Probably more than just that. She wrapped her arms around herself, shivering.

"We're going to stop this guy. I promise." Trent's reassuring words did little to reassure her. How could this be happening again?

A slow ache spread across her skull. She thought she'd finally come to terms with her sister's death. Now the nightmare was starting all over again and a man who'd had a part in her sister's death was walking free.

She racked her brain, trying to think if she should have seen the signs. Maybe if she'd paid closer attention, she would have realized something was wrong with him. And maybe her sister would still be alive.

"Stop," Trent commanded.

"What?"

"I can see what you're doing. Stop playing the what-if game in your head. This is *his* fault, not yours sweetheart. You have nothing to feel guilty about."

Too late for that. Even as she nodded, guilt assaulted her in potent waves, reminding her that she hadn't come through for her sister when she'd needed it most. She should have seen the signs. She'd worked with the man for God's sake. What if her rejection had pushed him over the edge? An involuntary shudder racked her body at the thought.

CHAPTER ELEVEN

Trent lay on his back staring at the ceiling. Sage lay next to him, curled up against his chest. Her breathing was finally steady but she'd been tossing and turning the past couple of hours. After dinner she'd been unusually quiet. He guessed she was blaming herself for what happened and wasn't surprised. After his time in the Navy, he'd seen enough people who dealt with survivor's guilt.

And she was pulling further away from him. He could see it in her eyes with every glance.

"Sage?" He shifted his body, feeling a little guilty at waking her when she'd finally dozed.

"Hmm?" Her head stirred against his chest.

"Sweetheart, I need to talk to you."

This time her eyes flew open. She pushed up on her elbow, her breast brushing against his chest. "Is everything okay?"

"Yeah." Even to his own ears, his voice came out hoarse and scratchy.

"What's going on then?" She laid her head back on his chest and threw a silky leg over him.

"Earlier you asked why I was helping you." In his thirty-two years on Earth he'd never said this to another woman but he had no doubt about how he felt. The words were foreign on his tongue but it was time to be honest. "I love you."

She shook her head, her hair brushing over his chest. "You don't mean that."

He expelled a deep breath. The woman was going to drive him mad. "I don't huh?" he murmured into her hair.

Wordlessly she shook her head.

"I looked for you in New York." The words cut through the air like a fifty cal sniper rifle.

She looked up now. "What?"

"When you disappeared, for the first time in my life I felt...lost. I'd been offered work up there and even though I knew it would be like looking for a needle in a stack of needles, I had to try." He'd never been this honest with anyone before and the feeling was fucking terrifying. Especially since she didn't appear to be reciprocating.

He could navigate across any terrain on the planet blindfolded, could kill a man twenty different ways and knew how to operate practically every type of firearm imaginable. Yet telling this sexy woman he loved her was the most intimidating thing he'd ever done. During his formative years, his mother had "loved" a lot of men, hence the fact that he and his brothers all had different fathers.

Hell, he'd never admitted to anyone, including Jason, why he'd stayed in New York as long as he did. The work had been steady but he could have come back to North Carolina anytime and done just as well.

Sage stared at him with those bright green eyes and everything inside him tightened. He couldn't read what was going on in that head of hers. Silently, she leaned forward and brushed her lips over his.

The movement was tentative at first, then she kissed him with an urgency he hadn't been expecting. Hell, he hadn't been expecting anything at all. He just wanted to get this off his chest so he could finally get some peace. And maybe a couple of hours of decent sleep.

Shifting, she straddled him but continued her greedy assault on his lips. Grasping her hips, he wanted to just plunge forward and impale himself inside her but managed to refrain. "Condom. Now," he ground out.

She leaned over and grabbed one from the drawer but she didn't make a move to put it on him.

If he didn't put one on now, he was liable to do something stupid. Not that he'd ever intentionally do something to hurt Sage. The only thing he cared about was being with her forever.

Forever. How could that word not scare him?

His Sioux ancestors had clear beliefs about certain souls being destined to meet. Until recently, he hadn't put much stock in it. Now he knew better. It wasn't a coincidence he'd found her again.

Her dark hair pillowed down around him as she kissed him. She rubbed her folds over the length of his cock but didn't take things any further.

The teasing was torture but something he gladly endured.

Since she seemed content to sit there all night, he palmed both of her breasts. In this position they fell perfectly into his grasp. She swatted his hands away as she delved lower, kissing his neck, then chest.

That was when he realized what she was doing and his chest swelled. She might not be ready or even able to tell him she loved him but this was about him right now.

Using her tongue, she swirled around his nipples, alternating back and forth before she trailed kisses down his stomach.

He loved the feel of her mouth on him. His cock throbbed so painfully all he could think about was flipping her over and mounting her but he restrained himself. If this was what she wanted to give him, he'd let her. Hell, he'd let the woman do damn near anything if it made her happy. Clutching the headboard above his head was the only way he could hold back from simply taking over.

Slowly, she raked her teeth over his abdomen, causing his entire body to go rigid. He was all for foreplay but he wanted her mouth on his cock like he wanted his next breath. Her hand fisted around his hard length as she looked up and met his gaze.

When she moistened her sensuous lips, he thought he'd die. With a mischievous smile, she bent over him, her dark hair creating a veil around her face. At first she flicked her tongue over and around the head of his cock, then she lightly blew her hot breath on him.

His hips jerked up, searching for release. Enough was enough. Apparently she understood he'd reached his limit because she cupped his balls and took him as deep as her mouth would allow.

Quickly, she fell into a rhythm. One that had him closer and closer to release. He slipped his fingers through her hair and lifted it back. He wanted to see her face as she worked him.

He groaned aloud when she shifted up higher on her knees to take him deeper. Her eyes were closed as she sucked and just when he felt his balls pull up impossibly tight, she slowed her movements.

She withdrew him from her warm mouth and licked down his length. Starting at the bottom of his shaft, she stroked up in one arousing motion before doing it again. And again and again.

"No more torture," he rasped out.

He could feel, more than hear the laughter come from her body as she leaned lower and sucked his balls into her mouth.

His entire body jolted at the sensation. Before he could reconsider, he scooted back, out of her grasp and grabbed the condom. Somehow he managed to roll it on without ripping it.

She sat back on her legs, watching him through veiled eyes. Her lips were pink and swollen and while he would love nothing more than to let her finish what she'd started, he needed to be inside her body.

"On your knees," he ordered.

Her eyes widened slightly but she did as he instructed. On shaky legs, she swiveled around and repositioned herself. He ran a palm over her smooth ass and an involuntary shudder raced through his body. The woman was pure perfection.

When he adjusted himself behind her, he tested her slickness with two fingers. Good. She was drenched and ready.

He pounded into her, loving the feel of his cock dragging against her tight walls. In this position he could go as deep as possible. She mumbled something he couldn't make out.

"What was that?"

"Harder." This time there was no mistaking her request.

He fisted her long hair, slightly tugging her head back. "Touch yourself." He was close to climaxing but he wanted her to find pleasure first.

Reaching around he tugged sharply on one of her nipples, earning a gasp of surprise, which quickly turned to a moan. Her tight sheath gripped him even harder.

As he'd instructed, she had one hand between her legs but her other gripped the sheet so tightly he could see the whites of her knuckles. He let her hair fall from his hands. It glided down her back like a silky waterfall.

He increased his movements, knowing she was close, felt it each time he thrust into her. Her sighs and moans mixed right along with his.

"Come on, sweetheart. Come for me." He needed her to come first.

There was so much he wanted to give her, it scared him. For a reason he couldn't put his finger on, tonight felt different. Like they were finally on the same page. Like she'd finally come to terms that she belonged with him.

"Trent," she moaned out his name as violent shudders racked her body. Now both her hands clutched the sheet as she writhed underneath him.

Her tight body clenched around his shaft so tightly, he lost it. His grunts and the sound of his balls slapping against her was now the only noise in the otherwise quiet room.

After what felt like forever, he emptied himself then collapsed forward, forcing her to do the same. He kept his weight on his arms though, not wanting to smother her. She shifted and twisted underneath him. His cock made a popping sound when it withdrew.

She maneuvered and flipped so that they were facing each other. "Trent." She paused before starting to speak again but he covered her mouth with his.

Whatever she was going to say could wait. It was too soon for her to return his feelings. He could deal with that for now.

She'd been running from her past for so long and now that she'd finally gotten settled somewhere, her nightmares had started all over again. The feel of her skin against his was the only thing he cared about at the moment. As long as she didn't run out on him again, he could handle anything.

"Get some sleep." He discarded his condom before falling back onto the bed.

She didn't respond but wrapped her arms and legs around him instead. Soon her steady breathing filled the quiet room. Once he was sure she was asleep he inspected the doors, windows and alarm system one more time. He didn't care that he was being paranoid. His system was nothing compared to the one she now had. Tomorrow he'd pack up his stuff and head to her place.

A quick glance outside eased his worry a fraction. Steve's cruiser sat next to the original cop car. Trent should have known Steve would do more than just a drive by. He'd probably stay staked out the entire night too.

Once he was sure everything was as secure as it could ever be, he chambered a round in his forty and laid it on the nightstand underneath an open book.

Then he let sleep finally overtake him.

* * *

Sage opened her eyes to the feel of a hand over her mouth. Immediately she went into fight mode. She started to struggle when she realized it was Trent.

When he saw understanding in her eyes, he removed his hand and placed a finger over his mouth.

She nodded. The house was quiet. Much too quiet.

And that was when it hit her. The room was dimly lit thanks to the stars and moon but the light from the digital clock on his nightstand was off. She couldn't hear anything else either, like the heater working.

Her stomach roiled. There wasn't a storm so someone must have cut the power.

Trent handed her a gun and using hand gestures, motioned she should go to the bathroom. Once they got to the entryway, he leaned down and whispered in her ear. "Don't come out for anyone but me."

She wanted to argue but knew it was impossible. Once inside, she threw on a discarded T-shirt and crouched down near the tub. The weapon felt foreign in her hands. After everything that had happened, she'd actually gotten a concealed weapons permit and had taken plenty of classes but she'd never gotten used to the feel of a gun.

And she'd prayed she'd never have to use it.

Light from the two small circular windows gave her enough illumination to see herself and make out shapes and figures in the room.

Her heart pounded mercilessly against her rib cage. Never before had she felt so helpless. She didn't know what Trent was doing, if he was even okay. Nothing.

If anything happened to him—no, she wouldn't think like that.

She should have told him how she felt about him earlier. The words had stuck in her throat though. Growing up, her parents hadn't been big on affection, so she'd learned from their example.

That was a lousy excuse though and she knew it. He'd manned up and told her how he felt. And something told her those few words had taken a lot for him to admit. Which made her feel worse, if that was even possible.

Gunshots reverberated through the house, jerking her back to reality.

She jumped to her feet and rushed to the door. For a moment she paused with her hand on the knob. He'd told her to stay put but if he was lying bleeding to death and she could have done something to stop it, she'd never forgive herself.

Easing open the door, she peeked outside. The room was empty. Hurrying, she tugged on a pair of sweatpants.

If she was going to be coming up against her stalker, she wasn't doing it half-naked.

Holding her breath, she opened the door to the hallway. Also empty. Though she wanted to expel a loud sigh, she held back. Shadows created grotesque figures down the hall leading to the stairs but she forced herself onward.

If Trent was hurt, maybe she could get outside. And why hadn't the cops responded anyway? They should have heard the shots.

Terror surged through her. Maybe they were dead.

Her feet were silent against the floor as she inched toward the stairwell. She could hear Trent's voice and it sounded like he was talking on the phone.

Still clasping her gun as if it was a lifeline, she rushed down the stairs. His voice grew louder and she could tell he was talking to the police now.

"Been shot...I need an ambulance...I don't know if they're all right...yes..."

She rounded the corner at the end of the stairs and crept toward the kitchen, toward Trent's steady voice.

"Trent?" her voice came out shaky.

His back was turned to her. Guarding the doorway with gun in hand, Trent was on the phone. But at least he was alive and unharmed.

He spared her a quick glance. "Sage. Don't come in here."

If he was able to talk, then he was fine. Ignoring his order, she continued toward the kitchen.

Peeking around Trent, she saw Graham Hartigan lying on the floor. A moonbeam illuminated his still figure. A big-ass gun was a couple of feet from his body and with the exception of the ski mask pulled back on his head, he didn't look scary.

His sprawled figure looked smaller than the man she remembered. He was only a couple of inches taller than her but on the floor and bleeding, he looked so non-threatening. She clutched her gun tighter.

"Is he dead?"

"Damn it, you shouldn't be in here."

"Where are the cops?"

"On their way. I don't know if Steve's okay though. He should have heard those shots."

"I'll go check on—"

"No. Stay behind me and don't move until reinforcements arrive. I'm serious." This time he met her gaze, his expression hard.

Nodding, she started to shift back when movement from her peripheral vision caught her eye.

The previously immobile man pulled something from behind his back. She didn't think. She just reacted. Trent lifted his gun but she couldn't take a chance.

Losing Trent was not an option. Using the full force of her body weight, she moved to tackle him.

He was faster though.

Realizing what she was doing, his arm shot out as he threw his body over hers, propelling her backward and into the hallway.

Loud booms erupted as they flew through the air. It was as if everything was happening in slow motion. A few bright flashes surrounded them and she was vaguely aware when something ripped through her shoulder.

When they hit the floor, pain fractured through her entire left side. She didn't know if it was from the fall or worse.

Trent rolled over her. "Damn it woman, what were you thinking."

When she tried to sit up, he hoisted her into his arms and rushed for the front door.

"What are you doing?" She tried to struggle in his arms but he held her closer.

"Getting you the hell out of here." As they stumbled into the front yard, two police cruisers, an ambulance and a fire truck, all with flashing lights zoomed up onto the lawn and into his driveway.

Men and women emptied from the vehicles and swarmed the house like locusts, brushing past them.

"What about him?" She didn't need to specify.

"He's dead trust me."

"How do you know?"

"Half his body is gone."

"What—"

"Son of a bitch rigged his body with explosives."

Holy shit! That's what that noise had been. She thought he'd had a machine gun or something. "Oh, God…" Words failed her then. Her throat clenched with pent-up tears but she held them back. If he could keep it together, she could too. At least for now.

He put her on her feet but gripped her shoulders. "Are you okay to stand?"

"I'm okay."

As she spoke, a blonde woman wearing an EMT uniform rushed up to them. "Is anyone hurt?"

She shook her head but Trent intervened. "I want her checked out."

The woman nodded and took Sage by the arm.

Sage turned to Trent. "Aren't you coming with me?"

"I need to find out if Steve is okay. He hasn't been responding to my calls."

Nodding at him, she allowed the other woman to lead her to the back of the ambulance. She hadn't realized how wound up she was but once she sat down near the rear door, she practically collapsed against the cool metal.

Her nightmare was over and Trent was alive and okay. And as soon as humanly possible, she was telling Trent exactly how she felt about him.

EPILOGUE

One Week Later

Trent opened the front door to Sage's town house and stepped inside. He shed his jacket and hooked it on the vintage coatrack. Familiar, appetizing scents teased his senses.

"Sage?"

"In the kitchen."

When he stepped into the bright room, he was almost disappointed to find her wearing clothes. Yesterday she'd been wearing an apron and nothing else when he walked through the door. After dropping a brief kiss on her lips, he collapsed onto one of the chairs.

Today she still wore the apron but it looked as if she was actually cooking. He motioned toward the stove. "Is that what I think it is?"

She grinned and his heart skipped a beat. He couldn't imagine ever getting tired of that smile. Something she seemed to be doing with more frequency. It was as if a weight had been lifted. Now she didn't have that lingering sadness in her eyes. "I hope it turns out okay but I've got a menagerie of stuff here. Blueberry Wojapi, frybread, wahu— okay, I'm not going to even try to pronounce it but they're basically corn fritters."

The correct term was Wahuwapa Wasna but he was surprised she even knew what it was. "How'd you learn to do all this?"

"Your mother." The words dropped like a grenade.

"My *what?*"

"She came by to visit Jason today at work and boy was she pissed when she found out you were living with a woman and she didn't know about it." Sage made a mocking tsk tsk sound before turning back toward the stove.

"My *mother* is in town?" Last he'd heard she was living in Vegas with a new boyfriend. At least she hadn't married this one. Not yet anyway.

"Yep. She said your father used to make this stuff all the time and that it was your favorite. She gave me the recipes… I hope it's okay, but I invited her to dinner tonight."

"What?" He knew he was practically yelling but he couldn't stop the raising pitch of his voice.

"How's Steve doing?" The little vixen ignored his question.

Standing, he moved to join her by the stove, sliding his arms around her from behind. He inhaled her sweet scent. "He's driving the hospital staff crazy but he's going to be fine." He'd been stabbed three times while doing reconnaissance around Trent's house but none of the wounds had proved fatal. He'd been knocked out cold for an hour before the paramedics arrived but since he didn't die immediately, they'd been optimistic he'd make it. Thankfully he had. The other officer hadn't been so lucky.

"Good. Now why don't you help me set the table in the dining room?" She nudged him with her elbow.

"Bossy much?" he murmured as he stepped away from her to pull plates down from one of the cabinets.

"You know you love it."

He did. He loved everything about her.

"Let me hear you say it," she demanded, laughter in her voice.

"Only if you say it first." Because that was the one thing he knew he'd never tire of.

"You know I love you." She turned back to the stove. "Even *your* annoying bossiness."

Plates set, he moved in behind her again, unable to keep his hands off her. He set his chin on the top of her head. "It's not a coincidence that we found each other," he murmured. "The Sioux believe all souls are on a journey and some are simply destined to meet each other no matter what you do or where you go in life. What happens when those souls meet, however, is up to the individuals."

She set down a long, wooden spoon and turned to him. "Free will and all that?"

"Yep. The future isn't written." But he knew his future was with Sage no matter what.

"Then I'm glad destiny gave us a second chance." Smiling, she wrapped her arms around his waist and laid her head against his chest.

He breathed in her scent and pulled her close. "Me too."

* * *

The End

Thank you for reading Dangerous Deception. I really hope you enjoyed it.

If you don't want to miss any future releases, please feel free to join my newsletter. I only send out a newsletter for new releases or sales news. Find the signup link on my website: http://www.savannahstuartauthor.com

COMPLETE BOOKLIST

Miami Scorcher Series
Unleashed Temptation
Worth the Risk
Power Unleashed
Dangerous Craving
Desire Unleashed

Crescent Moon Series
Taming the Alpha
Claiming His Mate
Tempting His Mate
Saving His Mate
To Catch His Mate

Futuristic Romance
Heated Mating
Claiming Her Warriors
Claimed by the Warrior

Contemporary Erotic Romance
Adrianna's Cowboy
Dangerous Deception
Everything to Lose
Tempting Alibi
Tempting Target
Tempting Trouble

ABOUT THE AUTHOR

Savannah Stuart is the pseudonym of *New York Times* and *USA Today* bestselling author Katie Reus. Under this name she writes slightly hotter romance than her mainstream books. Her stories still have a touch of intrigue, suspense, or the paranormal and the one thing she always includes is a happy ending. She lives in the South with her very own real life hero. In addition to writing (and reading of course!) she loves traveling with her husband.

For more information about Savannah's books please visit her website at: www.savannahstuartauthor.com.

Printed in Great Britain
by Amazon.co.uk, Ltd.,
Marston Gate.